D1442921

THE HOUSE ON WINDRIDGE

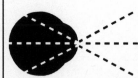

THE HOUSE ON WINDRIDGE

TRACIE PETERSON

THORNDIKE PRESS

A part of Gale, Cengage Learning

GALE
CENGAGE Learning·

Farmington Hills, Mich • San Francisco • New York • Waterville, Maine
Meriden, Conn • Mason, Ohio • Chicago

LIBRARY OF CONGRESS CATALOGING-IN-PUBLICATION DATA

Names: Peterson, Tracie, author.
Title: The house on Windridge / by Tracie Peterson.
Description: Large print edition. | Waterville, Maine : Thorndike Press, 2016. | Series: Thorndike Press large print Christian historical fiction
Identifiers: LCCN 2016021954 | ISBN 9781410491008 (hardcover) | ISBN 1410491005 (hardcover)
Subjects: LCSH: Large type books. | GSAFD: Love stories. | Christian fiction.
Classification: LCC PS3566.E7717 H685 2016 | DDC 813/.54—dc23
LC record available at https://lccn.loc.gov/2016021954

Published in 2016 by arrangement with Barbour Publishing, Inc.

Printed in Mexico
1 2 3 4 5 6 7 20 19 18 17 16

THE HOUSE ON WINDRIDGE

PROLOGUE

Windridge Ranch, Kansas
January 1, 1863

The pathetic cries of a newborn continued to split the otherwise heavy silence of the day long after the sheet had been pulled up to cover the infant's dead mother. The baby's hunger and misery seemed to feed her wails, despite the housekeeper's attempts to soothe and comfort the distraught child.

Gus Gussop had already borne the pain of hearing the housekeeper tell him his wife was dead. Now he faced the hopelessness of trying to satisfy a newborn — his wife's departing gift. Running his hands through his chestnut hair, Gus felt pain more acute than any he'd ever known. The tightening in his chest gave him cause to wonder if his heart had suddenly attacked him. He prayed it would be so and that he might join his beloved Naomi in eternal rest.

The baby's high-pitched cries intensified, causing Gus to storm from the room. "Find some way to shut her up!" he bellowed over his shoulder.

Slamming the door to the bedroom he'd shared with Naomi, Gus made his way downstairs to the front door. But he'd no sooner reached it than he heard the approaching footsteps of his good friend and ranch foreman, Buck Marcus.

"I'm deeply sorry for you, Gus," came Buck's apologetic voice.

"What do you want?"

"You can't be going out there now," Buck reminded. "Did you forget we're in the midst of a blizzard? Ain't no visibility for miles, and you'd surely freeze to death before you made it ten feet."

"Well, maybe I want to freeze to death," Gus answered flatly, turning to scowl at the red-haired Buck. "Leave me be."

Buck nodded at the order and took his leave, but when Gus turned back to the massive front door, he knew the man was right. For a few minutes, all Gus could do was stare at the highly ornate oak door — stare and remember. He'd paid a handsome sum to have the door designed with stained glass and detailed woodcarving. Naomi had been so very fond of pretty things, and this door, this entire house for that matter, had been Gus's gift to her for having a good nature about moving to the Flint Hills from her beloved home in New York City.

He turned and looked up at the beautifully crafted oak staircase. Wood came at a premium in Kansas. For that matter, with a nation at war against itself, everything came at a premium. But Gus had found ways around the inconvenience of war. The beautifully grained oak had been meticulously ordered and delivered over a two-year period, all in order to give his wife the best. The wood floors and heavy paneling in the library had been equally difficult to come by, but Gus had successfully managed each and every problem until he had exactly what he wanted for his impressive ranch house.

The house itself had been designed out of native limestone and stood atop the hill Gus had affectionately named "Windridge." They said the wind in Kansas was the reason that trees seldom stayed in place long enough to grow into anything worth noting. And while Gus had made his home on Windridge, or rather on the side of this massive hill, he was of the opinion that this was true. For miles around, they were lucky to find a single stubborn hedge tree or cottonwood. The rolling Flint Hills stretched out as far as the eye could see, and the only thing it was good for was grazing cattle.

Gus had built his empire, constructed his castle, married his queen, and now it all seemed to have been in vain. She was dead. Naomi had died in the house he had gifted her with upon their marriage, died giving birth to their only child.

"What do I do now?" Gus questioned aloud, looking up the stairs.

At least the baby had quieted. He had never once considered Naomi might die in childbirth. She seemed such a healthy, vital woman that to imagine her dead over something women did every day seemed preposterous. After all, they were only an hour away from Cottonwood Falls, and should there be any need for a doctor, Gus knew it would be easy enough to get one. But on the last day of the year, a blizzard had set in, making travel impossible. The storm had now raged for over twenty-four hours, and snow piled in drifts as high as the eaves on the house. The stylish circular porch was covered in ice and snow, and no one dared to set foot outside without a rope secured to him to guide him back to safety.

A line had been tied from the house to the barn and to the bunkhouse, but other than checking on the livestock, which had been crammed into every possible free spot in the barn, the men were ordered to stay inside, out of danger. This he could order and see performed to his specifications. But Naomi's labor was another matter entirely. It had begun in the midst of the storm and was so mild at first that Katie, their housekeeper, had thought it to be a false labor. But then Naomi's water broke, and Katie informed him that there would be no stopping the birth. The child simply would not wait until the storm abated.

Things went well for a time. Katie had attended many area birthings due to her experience growing up with a midwife for a mother. It didn't seem they had anything to worry about. But then the baby came breech, and Katie said the cord seemed caught up on something. She fought and worked her way through the birthing, praying aloud from time to time that she could save both mother and child. Standing at Naomi's side, offering what assistance he could, Gus had heard the prayers, but they didn't register. He still refused to believe that anything could mar the happiness he had shared together with Naomi.

But as the hours passed and he watched his wife grow weaker, he knew those prayers were very necessary. There seemed to be

11

nothing Katie could do to ease Naomi's suffering. She instructed the young mother-to-be, and Naomi heeded her, performing whatever task she was told to do. Katie had her out of the bed at one point to squat in order to push the child down. But nothing seemed to work the way it should, and Katie soon began saying things that Gus didn't want to hear.

"We may lose the baby," she had told him. "We may lose them both."

Gus had gone to the door then, just as he had a few minutes ago. He had planned to fight his way through the storm to the doctor's, if necessary. But one look outside, and Gus had known there was no hope of leaving Windridge. He prayed the storm would abate. Prayed his child might be born safely. But never did he pray that Naomi might not die. It was unthinkable that such a thing could happen. It simply didn't fit Gus's plans.

But the unthinkable did happen.

Shortly before midnight, Jessica Gussop arrived as a New Year's Eve baby. She cried out in protest as Katie lifted her from her mother's body. She cried in protest when Katie cut the cord, and she cried in protest when Naomi, after holding the child and kissing her tiny head, had died.

He could still see the look in Naomi's eyes. She knew she wasn't going to make it. She smiled weakly at Gus, told him she loved him — that she would always love him. Then she whispered Jessica's name and closed her eyes.

Gus shook his head, trying to force the horrible scene from his mind. It just couldn't be true. They were all mistaken. He would go back upstairs now, and Naomi would sit up in bed and call his name.

He reached for the banister.

It was possible. They could be wrong.

Sorrow washed over him, and he knew without a doubt there had been no error in judgment. Her presence was gone from Windridge. There was nothing upstairs for him now. Naomi's body was there, but not the lighthearted laughter, not the sweet spirit he had fallen in love with.

She would never sit up. She would never call his name.

He turned and walked away from the staircase and passed through large double doors that slid open to usher him into the walnut-paneled library. This had been his refuge and sanctuary whenever the events of the day proved to be too much. Now, it only echoed the sounds of his heavy steps as he crossed to the desk where he did his book work.

She was gone. There was nothing left. Nothing to hope for. Nothing to live for.

He pulled open a drawer and saw the revolver that lay inside. He could join her. He could settle it all with one single bullet. The idea appealed to him in a way that went against all that he believed. He had shared a Christian faith with Naomi, had served as an elder in the church at Cottonwood Falls, and had always remembered to give God the glory for all that he'd been blessed with. To kill himself would directly violate God's law but to live violated his own sensibilities.

Gus heard the cry again and knew that before he could settle his own affairs, he would first have to do something about the baby. Jessica. Naomi had called her Jessica, and Jessica she would stay. He hadn't cared much for the name — had teased Naomi, in fact, about calling any daughter of his by such a fancy name. Bible names were good enough for the Gussop family. But then Naomi had reminded him that Jessica came from the masculine root of Jesse — the father of King David. So it was to be Jessica for a girl and Jesse for a boy. Gus had liked that idea. He'd liked it even more when Naomi, the granddaughter of a highly respected preacher in New York City, told

14

him that Jesse meant "the Lord exists" and she liked very much to think that God would prove His existence through the life of this child.

"I see His existence, all right," Gus muttered. "The Lord giveth and the Lord taketh away." He refused to finish Job's ancient proclamation by blessing the name of the Lord.

"I can't raise a baby without a mother," Gus said emphatically. He slammed his hands down on the desk, then sent the contents flying with a wide sweep of his arm. "I can't do it! Do You understand!" he bellowed. "I won't do it!"

He shook his fist at the ceiling. "You can't expect me to do it without her. You can't be that cruel. You may give, and You may take away, but You can't expect me to be happy about it — to go about my business as if nothing has happened."

Silence. Even Jessica's cry had quieted. Gus looked down at the mess he'd made and slammed the desk drawer shut. First, he would see to the child. There would no doubt be someone who would take her and raise her to adulthood. Especially given the fact that upon his death, Jessica would inherit everything he owned. That would make her an attractive package to prospective parents. But who should he approach on the matter?

Katie, his housekeeper, was hardly the one to saddle with such a responsibility. At twenty-five, the thing that most amused Katie was Buck, and even though the man was thirteen years her senior, a May wedding was already in the works. No, it wouldn't be right to put Jessica off on Katie and Buck. Buck had been a friend to him long enough that Gus knew the man wanted no part of owning a big spread of his own. He'd told Gus on more than one occasion that if he died tomorrow he would be happy being Gus's hired man and friend.

Gus considered neighbors and friends in town, but no one struck him as having the right combination of requirements for raising his child. And those requirements were very important to him. Just because he didn't feel capable of seeing to the needs of his daughter didn't mean he wouldn't take those needs into consideration while choosing her guardian.

After several torturous days of thinking through all the possibilities, Gus had eliminated all names except one. Harriet Nelson. Harriet was the maiden aunt of his deceased wife. The woman had practically raised Naomi, and as far as Gus was concerned, she made the perfect choice for raising Naomi's daughter. But Harriet lived in New York City, and exchanging letters or even telegrams would take days — maybe months. Gus didn't like the idea, but it seemed his only recourse.

Then, too, Jessica was too young and sickly to travel. Katie had tried to find a proper source of nourishment for the child and had finally come up with sweetening and watering down canned milk. At least the poor babe could stomach the solution. Which was more than could be said for the other dozen concoctions that had been tried.

Taking pen in hand, Gus began the letter to Harriet. He explained the death of Naomi first, offering Harriet his condolences in recognition of her position as adoptive mother to his wife. Then he told her of Jessica. He described the child who'd been born with her mother's dark brown eyes, despite the fact that Katie had never heard of any infant being born with other than blue eyes. She also had her mother's dark brown hair, although there wasn't much of it. He described her as a good baby, telling of the trial and error in finding something to feed her. Then he concluded the letter by expressing his desire that Harriet take over the rearing of his daughter. He made no pretense about the issue.

I find that I am ill-equipped to care for an infant on a prairie ranch. The housekeeper has done a fine job, but with her own upcoming wedding, I hardly can rely on her for such assistance in the future.

Harriet, you are the only one to whom I would entrust this job. The reflection of your ability was clearly displayed in Naomi's character. I know you would raise the child to be a good Christian and to occupy herself with godly service. I know, too, that Jessica would be loved and pampered. Please understand, I am well aware of my own responsibilities. I would, of course, provide financially for the child and yield to your authority on matters concerning her schooling.

Please do not refuse me on this matter, Harriet. I know you planned a different life for Naomi, and apparently your choice would have been wiser. A Kansas cowboy and a prairie ranch were unworthy of a woman such as your niece, but I recognize my own limitations and would go so far as to say this is a matter of life and death. I would appreciate your speedy response on the matter.

Ever Your Faithful Servant,
Joseph Gussop

He reread the letter several times before finally sealing it in an envelope and penning the New York address on the outside.

There, he thought. *The job is done. I have only to mail this letter and receive her response and then — then I can put this all behind me.*

Buck came in about that time. "Boss, we've been looking things over as best we can. Looks like most of the stock survived."

Gus nodded. He had little desire to talk about the ranch or his responsibilities.

"There's something else I need to discuss with you," Buck said hesitantly.

"Then speak up," Gus replied, seeing Buck's apprehension. It wasn't like the man to skirt around an issue.

"It has to do with her."

Gus felt the wind go out from him. For days the only way he'd managed to get through the hours was to avoid thinking about her. It was one thing to mention her in a letter to Harriet, but another thing to consider what was to be done in the aftermath of her death. In fact, he had no idea what had already been done in the way of preparing her for her burial. He'd simply refused to have any part of it.

"All right," he finally answered.

"Well," Buck began slowly, "I built her, ah . . ." He faltered. "I mean, well, that is to say —"

"You built her a coffin?" Gus questioned irritably.

Buck nodded. "Yes sir. We took her out like you asked. But Gus, the ground is too froze up for burial."

Gus growled and pounded his fists on the desk. "I don't care if you have to blow a hole in the ground with dynamite. I want her buried today." Buck nodded and without another word took off in the direction from which he'd come.

Several hours later, Gus heard and felt the explosion that signaled the use of dynamite. It rattled the windows and caused the baby to howl up a fit, but Gus knew instinctively that it would also resolve the problem. They would bury her today. Buck would say the words, given their inability to have the preacher ride out from town, and they would put her body into the ground.

Gus tried to think of everything analytically. First he would see to Naomi. Then he would see to Jessica's care. Then he would take care of himself.

Two weeks after the little funeral, Gus was finally able to post his letter to Harriet in Cottonwood Falls. And two months after that, with a strangely warm March whipping up one of the first thunderstorms of the season, Gus rode back from town, reading the missive he'd received from New York City.

Of course, you must realize I am hardly the young woman I was when Naomi was small, but I would be honored to raise Jessica for as long as time permits.

He breathed a sigh of relief. She had agreed to take the child. He continued reading.

However, I do have my own requirements to see to such an arrangement. First, I desire final say over her upbringing. As you pointed out, you are hardly aware of her needs. I want no interference, no monthly visits, no constant trips back and forth between the desolate American desert and New York. I want the child to know proper society and schooling before she is exposed to the barbaric plains of

21

Kansas. I also believe it will diminish any sense of loss in the child. In other words, if she is constantly looking toward her next trip to Kansas, she may well be unruly and unwilling to focus on her life here.

Well, Gus thought, *that certainly wasn't a problem.* He wouldn't be around, but of course, he couldn't tell Harriet that.

Secondly, I have devised the figures that I believe constitute the proper amount of money necessary to care properly for a child in New York City. She will be a child of social standing, and, therefore, the cost is higher than you might otherwise believe necessary. If you will note the second page of this letter, however, you will see I have detailed the information for you.

Gus looked at the page and noted that Harriet had indeed outlined the cost for food, clothing, schooling, supplies, toys, furniture, and a nanny to assist Harriet. It all seemed perfectly reasonable, even if it was a pricey figure. *Still,* he thought, *it didn't matter.* He wouldn't be around to argue or protest Harriet's judgment. He turned back to the first page of the letter and continued to read.

If these things meet with your approval, then I will expect to receive the child whenever you deem yourself capable of delivering her.

Gus breathed a sigh of relief. It was all falling into place.

Once he'd arrived at Windridge, Gus called Katie and Buck into the library and explained the situation.

"I'm sending Jessica to her mother's aunt in New York City," he said flatly, without a hint of emotion in his voice. His emotions were dead. Dead and cold, just as she was.

Katie spoke first. "What? How can you do this? I'm perfectly happy to bring her up for you, Mr. Gussop."

"Katie," he replied, "you and Buck are about to begin your lives together. There's no need to be saddling you with a ready-made family."

"But we don't mind," Katie insisted.

"Honestly, boss," Buck added, and Gus would have sworn there were tears in his eyes.

"This is how it's going to be," Gus stated, leaving no room for further protest. "The Flint Hills is no place to raise a child. The desolation and isolation would be cruel.

There'll be no other children for her to grow up with, and the responsibilities of this ranch are enough to keep you both running from day to night. That is, unless you'd rather not stay on with me." Gus watched their expressions of sorrow turned to disbelief.

"Of course we'll stay on with you," Katie replied.

"Absolutely, boss. We're here to do our job but more important, we're here because we're friends."

Gus nodded. He would leave them both a hefty chunk of money upon his death. They were faithful and loyal, and a man didn't often find friends such as these.

"I have a favor to ask," he finally said. "I need Katie to take Jessica to New York. You can go along, too, Buck. Act as her escort. Miss Nelson is expecting the child, and the sooner we get started on it, the better. I'll go with you into town, and we'll purchase train tickets. I'll also draw out a substantial sum of money from the bank, and that will be your traveling money. I'll wire another substantial amount directly to Miss Nelson's bank account, so there will be no need for you to worry about carrying it with you. Will you do this for me?"

Katie broke down and started to cry, and

Buck put his arm around her. "Hardly seems like the kind of thing we could refuse," he told Gus. "But I can't leave Windridge right now. You know full well there's too much work to be done. Those Texas steers will be coming our way in another month or two, and that last storm took out a whole section of fence. Not to mention the fact that we're breaking six new stock horses. I can't take the time away and stay on top of this as well."

"It'll be here when you get back," Gus assured him.

"No sir," Buck said emphatically. "Katie's ma and brother can go along with her. If you'll pay their ticket instead of mine, I'd be much obliged."

Gus didn't like the idea but nodded in agreement. "If that's the way you want it," he told Buck.

"It is."

And so it was nearly a week later that Gus watched the carriage disappear down the long, winding Windridge drive. He felt strangely calm as he watched them go. He knew he'd done the right thing. The very best thing for all parties concerned. Jessica would grow up never knowing either parent, but she would be loved and cared for just as Naomi would have wanted.

With a solemnity that matched the weight of the moment, Gus turned and stared at the house he'd created. Three stories of native limestone made a proud sentinel against the open prairie sky. It was her house — her home. She had loved it, and he had loved her. The memories were painful, and for the first time since she had died, Gus allowed himself to cry.

At first, it was just a trickle of tears, and then a full rush of hot liquid poured from his eyes. He couldn't have stopped it if he'd tried, and so instead of trying, he simply made his way to the library and closed the door behind him. He thought for a moment to lock it but decided against it. Someone would have to come in and take care of the mess, and there was no sense in having them have to bust down the door and ruin the house in order to do so. The house would one day belong to Jessica, just as it had belonged to her mother. He wanted to keep it neat and orderly for her. He wanted to offer her at least this much of himself.

He took a seat at his desk and pulled out his handkerchief. Wiping away the tears, Gus took out a piece of paper and began to pen a note of explanation for Buck. He'd already seen to his will when he'd gone into

Cottonwood Falls for the train tickets. Everything would go to Jessica, with the exception of five thousand dollars, which was to be shared equally between Buck and Katie.

But this letter was an apology. An apology for not having been stronger. An apology for the problems he would now heap on his dearest friend.

I can't go on without her. The pain of losing her is too much to bear alone. If you can see your way to staying on and keeping up the ranch on Jessica's behalf, I would count it as my final earthly blessing. I have also arranged for you to be paid handsomely for the job. I just want you to know there was absolutely nothing you could have done to prevent this. I did what I had to do.

He signed the letter and left it to sit in the middle of his desk. He didn't want Buck to have a bit of trouble locating it. Then with a final glance around the room, Gus reached into the desk drawer and pulled out his revolver.

A knock on the library door caused him to quickly hide the gun back in its drawer. "Come in," he called.

Buck moseyed into the room as though nothing sorrowful had ever come to them. He held a pot of coffee in one hand and two cups in the other. "Thought you could use this just about now."

"I'm not thirsty," Gus replied.

"Well, then, use it to warm yourself."

"Ain't cold either."

Buck put the coffee down on top of the note Gus had just finished writing. He stared hard at Gus for a moment, then put the cups down and took a seat. "I can't let you do it, Gus," he said so softly that Gus had to strain to hear him. "I ain't gonna let you die."

Gus stared at him in stunned surprise. "What are you talking about?"

"I know what you're doing, and that's why I didn't go with Katie," Buck said, quite frankly. "I know you've been putting your affairs in order, and I know why."

Gus said nothing. He couldn't figure out how in the world Buck had known him well enough to expect this action.

"See, I know what it is to lose someone you love. You probably don't know this, but I was married a long time ago. I am, after all, thirteen years Katie's senior. Anyway, my wife died. Died in childbirth, along with our son."

Gus shook his head. "I didn't know that."

Buck nodded. "Well, it happened, and I would have followed her into the grave but for the ministerings of my ma. She knew how heartbroken I was. Sarah — that was my wife's name — and I had been childhood sweethearts. We'd grown up side by side, and we'd always figured on marrying. My ma knew it would be like putting a part of myself in that grave, and she refused to leave me alone for even a moment's time. And that's what I intend to do for you." He shifted back in the chair and crossed his leg to fumble with his boot for a moment.

"See, I know you intend to kill yourself, Gus. But it isn't the answer."

"I suppose you know what the answer is," Gus replied sarcastically. He wanted Buck to storm out of the room and leave him be. He didn't care if Buck hated him or called him names; he just wanted to forget everything and go to be with his Naomi.

"I do know," Buck replied. "God will give you the strength to get through this. You may not think so, but He will. I'm going to stay with you, pray with you, eat with you, and I'll even sleep at the foot of your bed if it keeps you alive."

Gus gave up all pretense. "I don't want to live. You should understand that."

"I do. But you're needed here on earth. You have a little girl who needs you. You have friends who need you."

"I don't want to be needed."

Again Buck nodded. "Neither did I, but I had no choice, and neither do you. Do you really want to leave that little girl with the guilt that she somehow caused her ma's and pa's deaths? It's bad enough that she'll have to live with the guilt of her mother dying, but hopefully, some kind person will teach her that it wasn't her fault. But if you put a bullet through your head, she'll be convinced it was her fault."

"That's stupid. It wouldn't have anything to do with her," Gus answered.

"You and I might know that, but she won't. And Gus, there won't be a single person in this world who'll be able to convince her otherwise."

Gus realized the truth in what Buck said. He felt his eyes grow warm with tears. "It hurts so bad to lose Naomi — to face a lifetime without her."

Buck nodded. "I know, and that's why we aren't going to face a lifetime. We're just gonna take one day at a time. I'll help you get through this, but you've got to be willing to try. For Jessica's sake, if for no other."

Gus thought about it for a moment. He

didn't have the strength to do what Buck suggested, but neither did he want to burden his child — her child — with the idea that she was responsible for his death. "I just don't know, Buck. When I think about the years to come — and I know that she won't be there — it just isn't something I want to deal with."

"I understand. But like I said, we don't have to think about the years to come. We only have to get through today," Buck replied. "And we'll let tomorrow take care of itself."

In that moment Gus chose life over death. His heart was irreparably broken, but logic won over emotions. One day at a time, Buck said, was all he had to face. Just one day. If life proved to be too much today, he could always end it tomorrow.

CHAPTER 1

October 1890

Jessica Albright wrapped her arms around her nine-month-old son and frowned at the dark-skinned porter. He held her small traveling bag and held out his arms to further assist her departure from the train.

"If it pleases ya, ma'am," he said with a sincere smile, "I kin hold da baby and hand him down to ya."

"No," Jessica replied emphatically. "No one is taking him."

The porter shrugged and then held up his hand. "I kin go ahead of ya. Then iffen you fall, ya'll fall against me." He smiled broadly and jumped down the steep steps ahead of her.

Jessica had no choice but to follow. She gripped the baby firmly against her breast and made her way off the train. The nine-month-old howled at the injustice of being held so tightly, and Jessica could only jostle him around and try her best to cajole him back into a decent temperament.

"Oh Ryan, neither of us is happy with the arrangements," she said, glancing from her son's angry face to the crowd gathered around the depot platform.

"Miss Jessica," a voice sounded from behind her.

Whirling around, Jessica met the smiling face of a snowy-haired man. "Hello, Buck. Thank you for coming after us. I'm sorry for having to put you out."

"Wasn't any other way you were going to get there, short of hiring someone in town to bring you out. Besides, Katie would skin me alive if I refused. This your little guy?" he asked, nodding at the angry baby.

Ryan continued to howl, and Jessica grew rather embarrassed from the stares. She felt so inadequate at being a mother. Where her friends in the city had spoken of natural feelings and abilities regarding their children, Jessica felt all thumbs and left feet. "Could we just be on our way, Buck?"

Buck looked at her sympathetically. "Sure, sure. Let me claim your baggage, and we'll be ready to head out."

"This here bag belongs to the missus," the porter announced. Buck took up the bag, but Jessica quickly shifted the baby and reached out for it. "It has our personal things." Buck nodded and let her take it without protest.

"I'll go for the rest." He ambled off in the direction of the baggage car, and Jessica felt a sense of desertion. What if he forgot about her? What would she do then? She had very little money with her and even less ambition to figure out how to arrange transportation to her father's Windridge Ranch. No, she thought, it was her ranch now. Her father had died, and there was nothing more to be said about the situation. Still, she'd only been here on three other occasions, and the last time was over five years ago. She'd never know which way to go if she had to figure a way home for herself.

Ryan finally cried himself out and fell asleep, but not until his slobbers and tears had drenched the front of Jessica's plum-colored traveling suit. She couldn't do anything about it now, she realized. Aunt Harriet had always said that a lady was known by her appearance. Was her attire in order? Was her carriage and walk upright and graceful? Jessica felt neither properly ordered, nor upright and graceful. She felt hot and tired and dirty and discouraged.

"Here we are. This all you brought?" Buck asked, one huge trunk hoisted on his back, a smaller trunk tucked under one arm, and a carpetbag dangling from his hand. He turned to include the young boy who followed after him with two additional suitcases.

"Yes," Jessica replied. "That's everything."

Buck never condemned her for the multiple bags, never questioned why she'd needed to bring so much. Buck always seemed accepting of whatever came his way. Jessica didn't know the man half as well as she would have liked to, but Buck was the kind of man she knew would have made a wonderful father.

Buck stopped alongside a mammoth, stage-styled conveyance. Jessica watched, notably impressed, as Buck gently placed the trunk and bags up on the driver's floor, then paused to hand her and Ryan up into the carriage. She arranged a pallet for Ryan by taking his blanket and one of the carriage blankets and spreading them out on the well-cushioned leather seats, while overhead Buck secured the baggage on top.

The opulence and size of the carriage greatly impressed Jessica. No expense had been spared. In fact, it very much resembled an expensive stagecoach of sorts. The beautifully upholstered seats sported thick cushions, leaving Jessica with the desire to join Ryan in stretching out for her own nap. After four days on the most unaccommodating eastern trains, she found this a refreshing reprieve.

Blankets were positioned on a rack overhead, as well as a lantern and metal box that she presumed held other supplies. Outside, she heard Buck instruct the boy to hand up his cases, then figured he must have tipped the boy for his actions when she heard the child let out a hearty, "Thanks, Mr. Buck."

"You all settled in there?" Buck called out, sliding a window open from where he was on the driver's seat.

Jessica thought the window ingenious and nodded enthusiastically. "I'm ready. The baby is already sleeping comfortably."

"All right, then. We'll make for home. I know my Kate will be half beside herself for want of seeing you again."

Jessica smiled weakly and nodded. She could only wonder at what her reception might be when they learned she was coming to Windridge to stay.

Since Buck had pulled shut the slide on the window, Jessica felt herself amply alone and reached inside her purse to pull out a letter. She'd only received the missive a week ago, but already it was wrinkled and

37

worn. Kate had written to tell her of her father's death. He'd suffered a heart attack, or so it was believed, and had fallen from his mount to his death. The doctor didn't believe he suffered overmuch, and Jessica had been grateful for that.

"We'd love to have you home, Jessie," the letter read. Kate was the only one who had ever called her Jessie. *"Windridge is never the same without you. Now with your father gone and what with the death of your own husband, we'd like to be a family to you. Please say you'll come for a visit."*

And she had come. She had telegraphed Kate before boarding the first available train, and now she was well on her way to Windridge.

But what would she do after that?

She stared out the window at the dead brown grass of the Flint Hills. She had felt fascinated the first time she'd laid eyes on the place at the age of twelve. Her aunt Harriet had figured it was time for Jessica to make a visit to the place of her birth; and sent west with a most severe nanny, Jessica had had her first taste of the prairie and rolling hills where thousands of cattle grazed.

And secretly, she had loved it. She loved the way she could stand atop Windridge when her nanny was otherwise preoccupied and let loose her hair ribbon and let the wind blow through her brown curls. She liked the feel of the warm Kansas sun on her face, even if it did bring her a heavy reprimand from her nanny. Freckled faces weren't considered a thing of beauty, not even for a child.

Now she looked across the vast openness and sighed. *I'm like that prairie,* she thought. *Lonely and open, vulnerable to whatever may come.* A hawk circled in the distance, and Jessica absently wondered what prey he might be seeking. It could possibly be a rabbit or a mouse, maybe even a wounded bird or some other sort of creature.

"Poor things," she whispered. Life on the prairie was hard. Often it came across as cruel and inhumane, but nevertheless, it continued. It went on and on whether people inhabited the land or died and were buried beneath its covering.

Jessica felt she could expect little more than this.

Her own life had taken so many different turns from that which she had expected. She had married against her father's wishes. But because he was a man who had never taken the time or trouble to be a real father to her, his hand-written letters of advice had held little sway with Jessica. After all, she scarcely knew her father. Harriet chose the man Jessica was to marry based on his social status and ability to conduct himself properly at social gatherings. It mattered very little that Jessica didn't love him. She was, Harriet pointed out, twenty-two years old. It was time to marry and take her place as a matron of society.

But society wasn't very accepting of you when you ran out of money.

High society was even less forgiving.

It grieved Jessica to know Gus Gussop had been right in his long-distance judgment of Newman Albright. Gus had called him a dandy and a city boy. Called him worse than that, as Jessica recalled. And Newman had been all of those things.

Harriet had died shortly after Jessica's marriage. With her death came the inheritance of a fashionable house and a significant amount of money. Newman refused to move them into the Nelson place. Instead he insisted they sell the place and buy a less ostentatious home. Jessica quietly agreed, having been raised to respect her husband's wishes as law. What she didn't realize was that Newman had managed to get himself deep into debt through gambling and needed the sale of the house to clear his ledgers.

He robbed her of both the fortune left to her upon Harriet Nelson's death and her father's wedding gift of ten thousand dollars. A gift Newman never bothered to mention. She found out about these things after Newman had died. Of course, by that time they were living in poverty, and Newman's only explanation was that Jessica's father had cut them off without a dime, and their investments had gone sour.

Upon Newman's death, Jessica learned the truth about everything. Things she'd much rather have never known. Part of this came by way of her father's request. Gus had sent a telegram asking her to be honest with him about her financial situation. When Jessica had given the pitiful statements over to her father via a long, detailed letter, Gus had written back in a livid anger that seemed to leap off the page and stab at Jessica's heart.

"That blackguard has robbed you blind, Jessica. He has taken the ten thousand dollars I wired to him, which was intended to go toward the purchase of a lovely new home, and has apparently wasted it away elsewhere. He's taken additional money, money he telegrammed requesting of me, and apparently

has lost the fortune given you by Harriet."

Jessica knew it was true. By the time Newman's death darkened her life, Jessica knew he had a gambling problem. A drinking problem. A fighting problem. And a multitude of other sins that had destroyed any possible hope of her loving him. He was a liar and a cheat and an adulterer, and Jessica could find no place in her heart to grieve his passing.

He had stumbled home one morning after an apparent night in the gutter not far from their poor excuse for a house. His nose was red, and his throat raw, and he bellowed and moaned about his condition until Jessica, then in her eighth month of pregnancy, had put him to bed and called for the doctor. Within three days, however, her husband was dead from pneumonia, and Jessica faced an uncertain future with a child not yet born.

It was at the funeral for Newman that Jessica realized the full truth of his affairs. Not one but three mistresses turned up to grieve their beloved Newman. None of the women had any idea about the others, and none knew Newman to have a wife and child. One particularly seasoned woman actually apologized to Jessica and later sent money that she explained Newman had given her for the rent. Jessica wanted to throw the money into the street but was too desperate to even consider such a matter. As a Christian woman of faith, she knew God had interceded on her behalf to provide this money. To throw it away would be to ignore God's answer to her prayers.

It had been painful to admit to her father that she was living from day to day in abject poverty, but even more painful to endure his response. He had raged about the injustice, but never once had he suggested she come home to live at Windridge. Jessica never even mentioned the baby to him. She was too afraid of what his reaction might be. Instead, she did as he asked, providing the information he sought on her finances. Then she followed his instructions when a letter came informing her that he'd hired a real estate agent to move her elsewhere and had set up an account of money in a New York City bank so that she might have whatever she needed. Such generosity had deeply touched her. But still, he never asked her to come home.

That broke her heart.

Then her life grew even more complicated when her best friend, Esmerelda Kappin, began to suggest Jessica give Ryan over to her for raising. Essie, as Jessica had once affectionately called her friend, was barren. She and her husband had tried every mid-wife remedy, every doctor's suggestion, and still they had no luck — no children. Essie took an interest in Ryan that Jessica didn't recognize as unhealthy until her friend began to suggest that Ryan preferred her care to Jessica's. Then Essie's very wealthy mother appeared on the doorstep to offer Jessica money in exchange for Ryan.

Of course, Jessica had been mortified and from that point on began guarding Ryan as though the devil himself were after the child. The Kappins grew more insistent, showing up at the most inopportune times to remind Jessica that she was alone in the world and that Ryan deserved a family with a mother and a father.

Jessica looked down at the sleeping boy. He did deserve a father, but that wasn't to be. She had no desire to remarry. Perhaps it was one of the reasons she'd decided to come to Windridge. Running Windridge would keep her busy enough to avoid loneliness and put plenty of distance between her and anyone who had the idea of stealing her son.

The prairie hills passed by the window, and from time to time a small grove of trees could be spotted. They usually indicated a spring or pond, creek or river, and because they were generally the exception and not the normal view, Jessica took note of these places and wondered if their gold and orange leaves hid from view some small homestead. Her father had once prided himself on having no neighbor closer than an hour's distance away, but Jessica knew that time had changed that course somewhat. Kate had written of a rancher whose property adjoined her father's only five miles to the south and another bound him on the west within the same distance. The latter was always after Gus to sell him a small portion of land that would allow him access to one of Gus's many natural springs. But Gus always refused him, and the man was up in arms over his unneighborly attitude.

Jessica wondered at her father's severity in dealing with others. Kate told her it was because he'd never managed to deal with life properly after the death of Jessie's mother. But Jessica thought it might only be an excuse for being mean tempered.

Her conscience pricked her at this thought. She didn't know her father well enough to pass judgment on him. Her Christian convictions told her that judgment was best left to God, but her heart still questioned a father who would send away his only child and never suggest she return to him for anything more than a visit. With this thought overwhelming her mind, it was easy to fall asleep. She felt the exhaustion overtake her, and without giving it much of a fight, Jessica drifted into dreams.

Her first conscious thoughts were of a baby crying. Then her mind instantly awoke, and Jessica realized it was Ryan who cried. She sat up to find the nine-month-old trying to untangle himself from the blankets she'd so tightly secured him inside.

"Poor little boy," she cooed. Pulling him from the confines of his prison, Jessica immediately realized his wetness.

Looking out the window, Jessica wondered how much farther it was to the house. She hated to expose Ryan to a chill by changing him in the carriage. Wrapping a blanket around the boy, Jessica shifted seats and knocked at the little window slide. Within a flash, Buck slid it open.

"Something wrong?" he asked, glancing over his shoulder.

"How far to the house?" she questioned.

"We're just heading up the main drive. Should be there in five minutes. Is there something you need?"

Jessica shook her head. "No, thank you. I'm afraid the baby is drenched, and I just wondered whether to change him in here or wait. Now I know I can wait and not cause him overmuch discomfort."

"Kate will probably snatch him away from you anyway. That woman just loves babies."

Jessica cringed. What she didn't need to face was yet another woman seeking to steal her child.

"Sure wish you'd told us about him sooner. Kate would have come east in a flash to help you out and see the next generation of Gussops."

She didn't bother to correct Buck by pointing out that the baby was an Albright. She thought of him as a Gussop as well. Despite the fact they both carried the Albright name, Jessica considered both herself and her son to be Gussops.

Buck left the slide open in case Jessica wanted to say something more, but she held her silence. She was nearly home, and the thought was rather overwhelming. *Home.* The word conjured such conflicting emotions, and Jessica wasn't sure she wanted to dwell on such matters.

"Whoa!" Buck called out. The carriage slowed and finally stopped all together. Jessica looked out and found they were sitting

47

in the wide circular drive of Windridge. The house stood at the end of a native stone walk, and it was evident that her father had sorely neglected the property in the last five years.

"Well, we're here, Ryan," she whispered against the baby's pudgy cheeks. "I don't know about you, but I'm rather frightened of the whole thing."

Ryan let out a squeal that sounded more delighted than frightened, and Jessica couldn't resist laughing.

Buck quickly came to help her down from the carriage, and just as he had predicted, Kate appeared to whisk them both inside.

"Oh my!" Kate remarked in absolute delight upon catching sight of Ryan. She reached arms out for the baby, but Jessica shook her head.

"He's soaking," she warned.

"Like that could stop me." Kate laughed and took the baby anyway.

Jessica felt a moment of panic, then forced herself to relax. *This is Kate,* she reminded herself. Kate, who had kept up correspondences over the years. Kate wouldn't try to steal her baby. Would she?

"What a beautiful boy!" Kate declared. "Come on. Let's get you in out of this wind and into a dry diaper."

Jessica glanced around and felt the breeze on her face. It invigorated and revived her. Somehow it seemed that city life had stifled her and drained her of all energy. Windridge had a way of awakening Jessica. It had begun with that first visit at twelve and continued with each subsequent trip home.

She finally looked back at Kate and found the woman was already ten feet ahead of her and heading up the stone steps to the porch. Drawing a deep breath, Jessica followed after the older woman, thinking to herself how very little Kate had changed. She now had a generous sprinkling of gray in her hair, and she wore small, circular, wire-rimmed glasses that gave her an almost scholarly appearance. But she was still the same old jolly Kate.

"You can see for yourself that the place has suffered miserably," Kate told her as they made their way into the house. "Your father wasn't himself for the last five years."

"Since my marriage," Jessica replied flatly, knowing full well that she had grieved him something terrible when she'd married Newman.

Kate stopped dead in her tracks. "Oh Jessie, I didn't mean it that way."

Jessica shrugged. "But it's true. I know it

hurt him. I wish I could take it back, but I can't."

"Don't wish for things like that," Kate admonished. "You'd have to wish this little fellow away as well. Everything comes with a purpose, and God turns even our disobedience into glory for Himself."

Jessica smiled. How good it felt to hear someone speak about God. Most of her friends in New York were into mystic readings and psychic adventures. They believed in conjuring spirits of dead loved ones and held all-night parties in order to satisfy their ghoulish natures. Jessica could have no part in such matters, even if the likes of such things were sweeping the eastern cities in a rage of acceptance.

She'd been told by a friend that Essie had purchased a charm to make Ryan love her more than Jessica. It was all madness, or so it seemed. Playing at what most considered harmless enchantments and magic spells had left Jessica desperate to find new friends. Friends whose faith was steeped not in manipulating people to do what they wanted but in seeking God and learning what He wanted.

"Did I lose you?" Kate asked, turning suddenly inside the foyer.

"Not at all," Jessica replied. "I was only

thinking of how wonderful it was to hear someone speak of God again. I'm afraid all manner of strangeness is going on in the city, and I've been rather alienated from good fellowship."

"You'll have to tell me all about it," Kate answered, and Jessica knew she truly meant it. Ryan began to fuss and pulled at Kate's glasses in irritated fashion. "Come on, little guy; let's get you changed."

Jessica felt a momentary panic as the baby continued to cry. She fought her desire to rip him from Kate's arms. It wasn't Kate's fault that Essie had treated Jessica so falsely. Swallowing her fear, Jessica followed Kate up the ornate wood stairs.

Focus on the house, she told herself. *Look at everything and remember how good it always felt to come here.*

Inside, the house looked much the same as it always had. Kate kept it in good fashion, always making it a comfortable home for all who passed through its doors. She was, for all intents and purposes, the mistress of Windridge, and she had done the place proud.

"We've created a nursery for you in here," Kate announced, sweeping through the open bedroom door. "Your room is in there." She pointed to open double doors

51

across the room. "Of course, you have access through the hallway as well."

Jessica looked around her in stunned amazement. A beautiful crib stood in one corner, with a cheery fire blazing on the stone hearth on the opposite side of the room. A dresser and a changing table were positioned within easy access of one another, and a rocker had been placed upon one of Kate's homemade rag rugs, not far from the warmth of the fire. There was a shelf of toys, all suitable for a baby, and yet another long oval rag rug on the floor where a small wooden rocking horse had been left in welcome. *No doubt,* Jessica thought, *Buck made most of the furniture, including the rocking horse.*

"It's charming here," Jessica said, noting the thin blue stripe of the wallpaper. "But really you shouldn't have gone to so much trouble."

"It wasn't any trouble," Kate replied, taking Ryan to the changing table. "I had kind of hoped that if I filled the place with welcome, you just might stay on." She looked over her shoulder at Jessica, her expression filled with hope. "We'd really like it if you'd give up the East and come home to Windridge. Would you at least think about it?"

Jessica nodded. "I've already thought about it. I had kind of hoped that you'd let me stay."

Kate's face lit up with absolute joy. "Do you mean it? You've truly come home for good?"

Jessica nodded. "If you'll have me."

Kate threw up her arms and looked heavenward. "Thank You, God. What an answer to prayer." She looked back to Ryan, who was now gurgling and laughing at her antics. "You're both an answer to prayer."

Jessica found her own room much to her liking. Delicate rose-print wallpaper accented by dusty rose drapes and lacy cream-colored sheers made the room decidedly feminine. Kate had told her earlier that the room had been designed for Naomi, and in spite of the feminine overtones, Gus had left everything exactly as Naomi had arranged it.

The massive four-poster bed was Gus's only real contribution to the room. It seemed a bit much for one person, but Jessica realized it had belonged to her parents and had always been intended for two. A writing desk was positioned at the window, where the brilliant Kansas sunlight could filter into the room to give the writer all possible benefit. A six-drawer dresser with wide gown-drawers was positioned in one corner of the room, with a matching vanity table and huge oval mirror gracing the space in the opposite corner. A chaise lounge of mahogany wood and rose print was the final piece to add personality to the room. Jessica could imagine stretching out there to read a book on quiet winter evenings.

The room seemed much too large for one person. But Jessica was alone, and she intended to stay that way. There seemed no reason to bring another husband into her life. How could she ever trust someone to not take advantage of her? After all, she was now a propertied woman — not just of a house, but of thousands of acres of prime grazing land. She would no doubt have suitors seeking to take their place as the master of Windridge. She would have to guard herself and her position.

But while she had no desire to bring a man to Windridge, she did want to bring people into her life. She wanted to share her faith and let folks see the light of God's love in her life. She didn't know exactly how she might accomplish this stuck out in the middle of the Flint Hills, but she intended to try.

After changing her clothes into a simple

black skirt and burgundy print blouse, Jessica checked on Ryan and found him still asleep. His tiny lips were pursed, making soft sucking sounds as he dozed. She loved him so much. The terror that gripped her heart when she thought of losing him was enough to drive her mad. Surely God would help her to feel safe again.

Jessica left Ryan to sleep and made her way downstairs. Her mind overflowed with thoughts about how she would fit into this prairie home, and she was so engrossed in figuring things out that she didn't notice the man who watched her from just inside the front door.

When she did see him, she froze in place on the next to the last step. Her heart began to pound. Was this some ruffian cowboy who'd come to rob the place? She forced herself to stay calm.

"May I help you?" she asked coolly.

He stood fairly tall, a good five inches taller than her own statuesque five feet seven. He met her perusal of him with an amused grin that caused his thick bushy mustache to raise ever so slightly at the corners. His face, weathered and tanned from constant exposure to the elements, appeared friendly and open to Jessica's study.

"You must be Jessica," he drawled as

though she should know him.

She bristled slightly, feeling his consuming gaze sizing her up. His cocoa brown eyes appeared not to miss a single detail. "I'm afraid you have me at a disadvantage," she finally managed.

"I'm Devon Carter, your father's foreman for these past five years."

Devon Carter. She thought of the name and wondered if anyone had ever mentioned him in their letters, but nothing came to mind. Buck had always been foreman over Windridge, but she knew he was getting up in years and no doubt needed the extra help.

"I'm Jessica Albright."

His smile broadened. "Good to have you at Windridge. Heard tell you have a little one."

"Yes," she replied and nodded. "He's upstairs."

"Kate has done nothing but talk about you and the little guy for days," Devon said with a chuckle.

Jessica stepped down from the stairs and folded her hands. It seemed fairly certain she had nothing to fear from this man. "Is there something I can do for you, Mr. Carter?"

"Devon."

She eyed him for a moment before nodding and saying, "Devon."

"I just came up to the house to talk to Buck about the feed situation. You don't need to pay me any never mind."

"I see." But in truth she didn't. Was this man simply allowed free run of the house? Did he wander in and out at will?

"Oh, good," came the sound of Kate's voice from the stairs. "You've already met. Jessica, this man was a godsend to us. Your father took him on as a foreman when Buck said the workload was too much, and he's quickly made himself an institution around here."

Jessica turned to find Kate coming down the stairs with Ryan. The baby appeared perfectly content in her arms.

"You do go on, Katie," Devon countered affectionately. "Say, he's a right handsome fellow. It'll be good to have him around. Keep us all on our toes."

"I won't let you change the subject," Kate said, coming down the stairs with Ryan. "Gus thought of you as a son. You earned his respect quickly enough."

Jessica felt her nerves tighten. Her father had never treated her with much respect, nor, as far as she was concerned, had he thought of her as a daughter. How dare this stranger come into her home and earn a place that should have been hers?

She quickly reached for Ryan as soon as Kate joined them in the foyer. She didn't want to feel angry or hurt for a past that couldn't be changed, but it bothered her nevertheless. How could these two people act so nonchalant about it, knowing full well that she had suffered from the separation?

"What with the fact you've spent all your life in the city," Devon said.

Jessica stared up at him, not at all certain what had preceded that statement. "What?"

"I just told Devon that you plan to stay on at Windridge and take over your rightful place as mistress of the ranch," Kate replied.

Jessica looked at Kate for a moment while the real meaning of her words sunk in. It was true enough that her father had left her the ranch, but she'd not thought much about the fact that by moving in, she would become the mistress in charge.

"And I was just saying I hoped our simple way of doing things wouldn't cause you to grow unhappy and bored, what with the fact you've spent all your life in the city."

"I assure you, Mr. Carter," Jessica said rather stiffly, "that I will neither suffer boredom nor unhappiness due to the location. Other things may well come about to make me feel those things but not the address of my new home."

With that she set off with Ryan to explore the rest of the house. She felt an awkward silence fall behind her and knew, or rather sensed, that Devon and Kate were staring after her, but she didn't care. She wasn't prepared for the likes of Devon Carter. And she certainly wasn't prepared for her reaction to him.

CHAPTER 2

At thirty-two, Devon Carter was pretty much a self-made man. He held deep convictions on two things. One, that he loved Windridge and the Flint Hills as much as any man could ever love a place. And two, that his faith in God had been the only thing to sustain him over his long years of loneliness and misery.

He dusted off his jeans, wiped his boot tops on the back of each leg, and opened the back door to the kitchen without any announcement. He found Kate busy at work frying up breakfast and crossed the room to give her an affectionate peck on the cheek. Kate had become a second mother to him, and he saw no reason that their closeness should end now that Jessica Albright had come home to claim her fortune, if one could call it a fortune.

"Morning, Katie."

"Morning, Devon. Did you sleep well in

the garden house?"

"It was good enough," he replied. "Don't know how you and Buck ever managed to keep warm enough out there, what with the drafts and such."

"We had each other," Katie said with a grin. "Besides, nobody's lived out there in twenty years. Gus had us move up to the house when the quiet got to be too much. We brought the kids and all, and he never once complained about the noise."

"Well, I'm going to have to do some repairs to it today if I'm going to have a better sleep tonight."

"Why don't you just tell Buck what you need? That would be simple work for him, and I don't want him overdoing it by following you over the prairie searching for strays. He just doesn't have it in him anymore."

"Now, Katie, you're selling me short again," Buck announced as he came in from the pantry.

"Just being sensible," Katie replied, pausing long enough to turn over a thick ham steak from where it browned in a cast-iron skillet.

"Well, sensible or not," Devon replied, "the work still needs to be done. You want the pleasure, Buck, or shall I do it?"

Buck laughed, watching Kate pull down her wire rims just far enough to look at him over the tops. "I'll take care of it. You just give me some ideas on where to start."

"Will do." Devon turned then to Kate. "Table set?"

"Nope, you go right ahead and do the honors. Buck and I will bring in the food."

Devon nodded and went into the pantry where the fine china and everyday dishes were displayed in orderly fashion. He took down three plates then remembered Jessica and Ryan, as if he hadn't thought of them all night long, and added one more. He grabbed silverware and saucers and decided to come back for the cups after seeing that he was juggling quite a load.

He'd just finished laying out the arrangement and filling the saucers with cups when Jessica and Ryan appeared. She stood casually in the doorway, baby on her hip, looking for all the world like a contented woman. Devon smiled.

"Breakfast is nearly on."

She looked rather surprised as she took sight of the table. "Who else will there be?"

"Well, there's Buck and Kate," he answered, then added, "and me. Plus you and Ryan. That makes five."

"Oh," she answered, and Devon immediately wondered if she had a problem with the arrangement.

"Something wrong?" he asked.

"I'm just not used to . . . well, that is to say . . . ," she fell silent and shifted Ryan to the other hip, where he found her long chestnut braid much easier to play with.

"Jessie," Kate called out as she brought in a huge platter of scrambled eggs, "my, but don't you look pretty. I like that you've left your hair down. Reminds me of when you were a little girl."

Devon watched Jessica blush as Kate continued. "Do you know, Devon, this girl would defy her nanny and sneak out of the house to get to the top of the ridge. Once she got there, she'd pull out all her ribbons and whatnots and let her hair go free to blow in the wind. Anytime she got away from us, we could be sure to find her there."

Devon grinned and cast a quick glance at Jessica, who was even now trying to help her son into the wooden high chair at the end of the table.

"Here, let me help," Devon said, pushing Jessica's hands away. He made a face at Ryan as he positioned the boy in the seat and brought the top down around him. Ryan immediately laughed and reached out chubby arms to touch Devon's mustache.

"No, Ryan!" Jessica declared, moving back in position to keep her son from touching the cowboy.

"It's all right, Jessica. He won't hurt anything," Devon replied.

She glared hard at him. "I'm his mother, Mr. Carter. It's my place to decide what is right for him."

Devon saw the unspoken fury in her eyes, but rather than angering him, it made him want to laugh. *Better not,* he told himself. *That would really infuriate her.*

He waited until Jessica took her seat at the right of the high chair before considering that he'd positioned himself at the left. He liked kids. Liked them very much and had, in fact, planned on having several by this time in life. But life often didn't work out the way a person planned.

Katie and Buck took their places, and Buck offered grace over the food. He also added thanksgiving for Jessica's return, before putting on a hearty "amen" and directing everyone to dig in. If Jessica noticed that Buck was the one in charge of the meal, she didn't say anything. She sat opposite Buck at the end of the table, while Katie sat at his right and Devon at her right. One entire side of the table sat empty except for the food platters, and Devon wondered if maybe he should have arranged things differently. He was about to speak when Buck voiced a question.

"How did you sleep last night, Jessica?"

She put down a forkful of fried potatoes and smiled. "Very well, thank you."

"I told him a person could get lost in that big old bed of your pa's," Katie said, "but you know Buck. He said we could always send out a search party to find you."

They all chuckled at this, and Devon wondered if maybe the tension of the morning had finally subsided.

"Ryan also slept very well. In fact, it was his first time to sleep through the night without waking up to . . ." She reddened and stopped in midsentence.

Kate seemed to understand her discomfort. "He's a big boy now. Have you started him eating something more substantial?"

Jessica shook her head. "No, in fact, this is his first time at the table."

She hadn't noticed, but Devon had put several pieces of egg on the high chair tray, and already Ryan was stuffing them into his mouth.

"Well, it looks as though he thinks highly of the idea," Buck said with a laugh.

Jessica looked down in confusion and noticed the baby reaching for a piece of buttered toast. "No, Ryan!"

"He's fine, Jessica," Devon assured her.

"Mr. Carter, I don't appreciate your interference with my child," Jessica said harshly. "He's my responsibility."

"Around here, folks pretty much try to help out where they can," Devon countered, meeting her haughty stare. "I figured since you're staying on, I'd try to do what I could to fill in for the absence of his pa. I'm sure Buck feels the same way."

Jessica appeared speechless. She stared openmouthed at Devon and then turned to Kate and Buck. "And you think this is acceptable behavior?"

Kate laughed. "We don't hold any formalities around here. Ryan will be greatly loved and maybe even spoiled a bit, but those are good things, not bad. The ranch is full of dangers as well as benefits. You'll appreciate that folks are willing to keep an eye open for him."

"No, I'm not sure I will," she replied quite frankly.

"Jessica, you shouldn't worry about these things," Kate told her.

Devon watched her reaction and tried to pretend he was unconcerned with her hostility. But in fact, he was offended that she should be so put out with him. He was, after all, only helping. Maybe it was her upbringing that caused her to be so mulish about things.

"I'd appreciate it if we could change the subject," Jessica interjected. "And, I'd appreciate it, Mr. Carter, if you would leave the raising of my son to me."

Devon swallowed back a short retort and let it go. There would no doubt be time enough to take issue over these things. He felt deep gratitude when Buck did as Jessica requested.

"Well, since you've decided to stay on, Jessica, there are a few things you need to be aware of."

"Such as?" The woman's eyes were wide with a mixture of what appeared to be fear and pure curiosity.

Buck looked at Kate for a moment, and after receiving her nod of approval, he began what Devon knew he dreaded more than anything.

"It has to do with the financial affairs of Windridge."

"I see." She busied herself with her food, and when Ryan cried for another piece of toast, she calmly buttered one and broke off a piece for him.

"Well, anyhow," Buck continued. "Windridge is not in a good state. Gus got into

67

drinking these last few years. About the time you . . ." He fell silent.

"Married Newman," Jessica filled in for him.

"Yes, well, when you got married, other things started happening around here as well. Your pa suffered a mild heart attack, and we had a round of viruses that took the lives of most our herd one year. One thing after another took its toll, and before we knew it, Gus was running pretty short on cash. After that, he just stopped trying. Wouldn't even keep up his partnership with the Rocking W down in Texas."

Jessica dropped her fork. "What partnership?"

Kate leaned forward to explain. "Your pa had an agreement to purchase cattle from a ranch in Texas. It was easier to get them that way, fatten them up here all summer, then sell them off in the fall — usually for a good profit. That way, we didn't have to worry about keeping them through the winter."

"I suppose that makes sense," Jessica agreed.

"Well, for the last three years or so, Gus let things get so far out of control that he couldn't even afford to purchase the steers. Jeb Williams, owner of the Rocking W, offered to spot him the herd. He knew Gus was down on his luck and knew he was good for the money, but Gus refused. He became more and more reclusive, spending most of his time nearby, but doing little or nothing."

"So you're telling me that we're broke?" Jessica questioned.

"Pretty much so," Buck replied. "Devon can give you better details on the matter."

She looked to him, and Devon thought from her expression that it had cost her a great deal to put aside their differences to pose her question. "What exactly is the situation, Mr. Carter?"

"There's not much in the bank. It'll get us through another winter, if the winter isn't too bad. There's only minimal livestock — a dozen milk cows, about the same number of horses, and the place is in a state of disrepair. We've tried to keep up with things, but it takes money to do so. Come spring, we'll be in a world of hurt."

"But I see cattle on the hills," Jessica replied. "Kate, you even mentioned the hands would soon be driving the cattle to Cottonwood Falls."

"They aren't ours," Devon told her instead of allowing Kate to answer. "We leased out the pasture without telling Gus. He mostly stayed in his room those last few months, and if he noticed the herd, he didn't say anything. The lease money is what we have in the bank."

"What are we to do?" Jessica asked, turning her gaze back to Buck and Kate.

"Well, there's a neighbor, Joe Riley, who'd like to buy a parcel of land that joins his property. It has a spring on it, and he's been after your pa for all these years to let him buy it. Your pa just felt mean about it, I guess," Buck replied. "Never did fully understand why that man refused to sell one little spring, but that's behind us now, and I don't intend to speak ill of the dead. He probably won't be interested until spring, but it's worth asking about."

"Then I thought I'd go down to the Rocking W on your behalf," Devon said rather cautiously. "I know Jeb Williams from the cattle drives I've helped with before coming to Kansas. I think Jeb might be willing to extend the same offer to you that he offered to your father. We could purchase a small herd from him — on credit — and fatten them up for a profit come fall."

"Of course," Buck threw in, "there's always a risk. Viruses, weather, insects, and all other manner of complications. It could end up that we'd lose our shirts in the deal and be unable to pay Williams back."

Jessica nodded, appearing to consider the matter. "I have an idea for the place," she said, surprising them all. "Back East, there is quite an interest in ranching and the West. Many people have never known much but the city — especially those in higher social classes."

"And your point would be?" Devon asked.

"My point is that opening resort ranches has become quite popular. They offer an unusual respite for travelers who otherwise live their lives in big cities. I have a couple magazines upstairs that talk about this very thing."

"Dude ranches," Devon said in complete disgust. "Your pa would sooner you sell the place in total."

"My father isn't here," Jessica reminded him. "And it appears that even when he was, he wasn't much interested in what happened with the ranch. The place is mine now, and I intend to run it as such. I realize I have a lot to learn, but I'm offering one simple solution. People could come here and take their rest. We have miles of solitude to offer them. We could feature carriage rides, hunting, picnics, and horseback riding — we could show them how a ranch actually works, and we could fatten them up on Kate's cooking."

"You forget," Devon replied, "the place would have to be fixed up first. There's a lot that needs to be done in order to make this a model working ranch. And that, my dear Jessica, takes money."

She frowned at him. "I realize it would take something of an investment to get things started. I didn't say the plan was without challenges."

"A plan? So do you figure to just move forward with this plan? Didn't you think it might be important to get the advice of those who know the place?" Devon questioned.

Kate and Buck stared on as if helpless to interject a single word. Jessica slammed down her empty coffee cup and countered. "I am not stupid, Mr. Carter. I am simply offering the idea up as a possibility. That is all." She glanced to Kate. "I also believe it would be nice to open the ranch up to hurting souls. People who need the quiet to escape and heal from whatever woe they have to face. As Christians we can minister to these people and share the gospel of Christ."

"Now you're suggesting we turn this into some sort of revival grounds?" Devon asked.

"And what if I am? Are you a heathen,

Mr. Carter?"

"No ma'am. I accepted Christ as my Savior a long time ago, but I never once felt called to be a minister."

"Neither have I called you to be one, Mr. Carter." She stressed the formality of his name, and Devon cringed inwardly.

Ryan pounded the tray with his hands and fussed for something more to eat or play with. Devon handed the baby a spoon without even realizing what he was doing. Jessica scowled at him and merely took the spoon out of Ryan's hands. This caused the baby to pucker up, and as his bottom lip quivered, he began to cry.

"Now, do you see what you've done?" she snapped at Devon.

"I didn't make him cry. You're the one who took his spoon away."

"Ohhh," she muttered and handed the spoon back to Ryan. "You and I are going to have to have a more private discussion of this matter, I can see."

"You name the time and place," Devon countered, feeling completely up to any challenge Jessica could offer.

"The point is," Buck finally interjected, "Windridge is going to need some help. Arguing about it isn't going to make improvements around here."

"I think if we sink our remaining capital into spring stock," Devon replied, "we could have enough to sell off next year and make a good profit. Beef sales are doing just fine. The immediate need is for us to build back our capital — not to spend it on frivolous ideas that might never come to be worth anything."

"I disagree," Jessica replied. "And since I now own Windridge and you are just the hired help, I believe I have the final say."

Gasps from Kate and Buck came at the words *hired help,* but Devon held his temper in check. "I may be the hired help, but I was hired because I knew ranching. Your father thought enough of my skills to honor me with his trust. I think that should say something for itself."

"It says plenty, and so does the rundown state of this ranch. If you are such a good foreman, Mr. Carter, why do I arrive to find the place in such a state?"

Kate put a hand on Devon's arm. "Jessie, you don't understand all that has happened. Devon had little say about matters of finance. He is a good foreman for the ranch, knows cattle and horses, and is handy with repairs, but he didn't have any say over the money. Your father was the one who made all the decisions — bad and good."

"And he's gone," Jessica said simply.

"Not if you just pick up where he left off," Devon proclaimed without thinking.

Jessica stared at him for a moment. "I resent that implication, Mr. Carter. And I would further add that if you don't like the way I intend to do things and if you think it impossible to take my orders seriously, then I'd suggest you find another place of employment."

"No, Jessie!" Kate declared. "You don't even know what you're saying. Now I want both of you to calm down and stop acting like children. A ranch takes a lot of people to see it through. We can work at this together and build it up, or we can destroy it. It's pretty much up to us."

Jessica seemed to take heed of Kate's words and fell silent.

Devon threw down his napkin and got up from the table. "I have work to do," he announced and stormed out of the room. *Aggravating woman,* he thought. *Thinks she can just come in and solve the problems of the world by forcing us all into her mold.* He slammed the kitchen door behind him as he made his way into the crisp October morning.

Glancing skyward, he prayed. *Lord, I don't know why this has to be so difficult. I figured her visit would be trying, what with her being a city gal and all, but I didn't figure on her turning this place into a dude ranch. I need some help here, Lord.* He looked out across the broken-down ranch and sighed. *And I need it real soon.*

CHAPTER 3

Winter moved in with a harshness that Jessica had not expected. Living near the top of a high ridge caused them to feel every breeze and gale that came across the prairie. It also made them vulnerable to the effects of that wind.

Jessica tried not to despair. She knew that any plans she had for the ranch would have to wait until spring, so she tried to busy herself around the house. Her friendship with Kate also blossomed as the women worked together. Kate gave Jessica her first lessons in canning, butchering, and quilting, and out of everything she learned, Jessica thought quilting to be the very best.

"I think quilting is the only way to make it through the long, lonely winters," Kate told her one afternoon. "I've passed many a winter this way."

Jessica stared at the quilt block in her lap and sighed. "I just wish I was a better seamstress. My stitches are so long and irregular. I'm sure I shall never be able to make anything useful."

"Nonsense. We all had to start somewhere. You do a fine job embroidering, and if you have a way with a needle, you can certainly learn to quilt."

"What do you do with all the quilts you make?" Jessica asked.

"I give them to family, use them here, or just stack them up in the storage room."

"I'll bet folks back East would pay good money to have a beautiful quilt like that one," she said, pointing to the quilt frame where Kate worked.

"This old flower basket pattern isn't that hard. Most folks could whip one up for themselves. Can't imagine they'd pay much of anything for my work."

"But they would. I have several friends in New York who would be very happy to purchase something like this. They don't sew — in fact, they're worse than me when it comes to putting in a stitch. They love beautiful things, and your quilts would definitely fall into that category," Jessica protested.

Kate stopped in her tracks. "You honestly think folks would pay good money to buy my quilts?"

"I do," Jessica replied enthusiastically. "Kate, if you were willing to part with some of your quilts, I could ship them back to my friends and see what kind of money they could raise. They could send the money, as well as some additional materials, and maybe if they talked to their friends and families, they would have orders for additional quilts."

"That might be one way we could raise some money for the ranch," Kate replied. "Of course, it wouldn't be like selling off a steer, but every little bit would help. Especially after so many years of waste."

Jessica paused and grew thoughtful. "Kate, what happened with my father? I mean, what caused him to start drinking?"

Kate stopped her work and looked sympathetically at Jessica. "I can't really say. I know he was never the same after Naomi died. He loved that woman more than he loved life. Buck feared he'd kill himself just in order to be with her. He just lost all desire to go on, and we did our best to keep him among the living."

"But he seemed so capable whenever I came to visit. And the ranch, I mean, it never looked like this."

Kate's expression took on a sorrow that immediately left Jessica feeling guilty.

"Your father had a number of things happen to put him into despair. The losses were just too much for him to bear."

"What kinds of losses?" Jessica dared the question, fearful of what the answer might be.

Kate pushed up her glasses and set her attention back on the quilting. "He lost a great deal of money, for one thing. I'm not really sure where it all went. I know he gave everyone a bonus, and when hard times came, we tried to give it back, but Gus wouldn't hear of it. Buck and I just gradually added it back into the purchases we took on for the ranch. Gus was always helping one friend or another out — never thinking that the money might not be there in the future.

"Then that summer, half the stock came down sick and died. That caused all kinds of problems. Drought came on us later that same summer, but we still had the freshwater springs, so we didn't suffer for water like most folks. Just when things seemed to be getting a little better, a late summer storm set the prairie on fire and burned most everything in its path. The bad thing was, it wasn't just one fire, but a series of fires, and the cattle and wild critters had no place to run. For some reason we'd neglected plowing fire strips — those are wide breaks in the prairie where we don't allow anything to grow. They can be very useful in containing fires because when they reach those places, the fires just sort of burn themselves out. But that year we just didn't see to it properly.

"The fire killed whole herds in some areas. We spent over forty-eight hours toting water up from the springs and watering down everything in sight and plowing wide strips around the main homestead. We were able to save the house and most all the outbuildings, but nothing else. The house smelled like smoke for months afterward. We lost so much that I thought Gus was going to up and sell it off for sure. But he wouldn't sell — felt it was too important to stay on."

"Why?"

Kate shook her head. She seemed reluctant to speak. "I think Gus worried about all of us. You, included."

"Worried? In what way?" Jessica couldn't imagine that this powerful figure she'd always known as her father would be worried about anything.

"He worried about whether we'd be cared for. He worried about Buck and me having a place to live. He worried about you back East with that money-grubbing social dandy." Kate stopped and threw Jessica an apologetic look. "Sorry. I shouldn't have said that."

Jessica sighed and shook her head. "Why not? It's the truth. Might as well tell it like it is."

Kate turned up the lantern a bit, then went back to work. "Well, he worried about you. He always feared that sending you back East wasn't the right thing to do, but you must understand that he felt so inadequate to deal with you."

"Is that why he sent me in the first place?" Jessica asked flatly.

Kate halted her work and pushed away from the quilt frame. "Jessie, I know we've never really talked about any of this, but with your father gone, I figure it's all right to talk about it now."

"Then please do," Jessica encouraged.

"Your father intended to send you off to your aunt, then kill himself."

"What?"

"You heard me. He totally broke down with Buck and told him he had no desire to live. Buck had been your father's friend long enough to realize that he would feel this way. He stayed with your father through the next months. Sometimes he even slept in the same room with Gus — on those nights that were particularly bad. Buck would make a pallet on the floor of Gus's room and keep watch over him until he fell asleep. Those were usually anniversaries. You know, her birthday, her death day, their wedding day. Those were the worst for Gus."

Jessica nodded. It was easy to imagine the pain and suffering that those simple reminders must have put upon her father. It seemed funny that where Newman was concerned, Jessica felt only relief. Sometimes it made her feel guilty, but most of the time she was just glad to be rid of him. She tried not to hate him, because hating him seemed to make it impossible to love Ryan in full. And she wasn't about to jeopardize her relationship with Ryan. He was all she had, and no one would take him from her.

"When you married," Kate began again, "your father feared for you. I remember him hiring a man back East to send him a report on Newman's background and financial status."

"He did what?" Jessica questioned.

"He hired a man to check into Newman Albright. The reports that came back weren't at all flattering."

"He knew about Newman?" Jessica questioned, completely mortified that she'd not been able to hide the details of her married life from her father. She'd known that her father was aware of the gambling and the financial crisis Newman had heaped upon his family, but surely he didn't know about the mistresses and other problems.

"He knew it all. The women, the abuses, the baby. He made me promise to never say anything to you in my letters. It worried him sick sometimes. He used to talk to me about it — ask my advice. I told him if you felt like talking, you'd do it."

"But he never showed me any sign that he'd be open to my talking to him," Jessica replied angrily. "Even when he knew me to be widowed, he never asked me to come home."

"But you never gave any indication that you would have wanted to come home. You stopped visiting, even though you were old enough to make your own decisions. You up and married without even asking him what he thought —"

"Why should I have asked him?" Jessica interrupted. "He'd barely showed the slightest interest in my life."

"That's not true, Jessica. Your father had detailed monthly reports from your aunt Harriet. It was her rule that you not be allowed to come to Windridge before you reached twelve years of age."

"I didn't know that," Jessica replied, her anger somewhat abated. "I thought he didn't want me here. I mean, he's the one who sent me away."

"He sent you because he planned to end his life. Then when he finally had a reason to go on, you were well established with your aunt, and to force you to a life out here on the Kansas Flint Hills seemed cruel. Besides, he'd signed an agreement with Harriet. Your father, if nothing else, was a man of his word."

"Would he have really asked me to come here? If Aunt Harriet would have been willing, would my father have brought me home?"

Kate shrugged. "Who can say? We have no way of reliving the past to see what other choices we might have made. You have to stop worrying about what might have been and focus on what is. You have a fine son and a failing ranch. It's the future that needs your attention."

"I realize that, but sometimes the choices for the future find their basis in the past," Jessica replied.

"True. I guess I can see the sense in that."

"Well, you ladies are gonna freeze to death if you don't stoke up that fire," Buck said, coming into the room with an armload of firewood. "I just put more wood on the fire in the baby's room."

"Is Ryan still asleep?" Jessica questioned.

"Yup. He didn't even stir," Buck replied. He put several thick logs into the massive stone fireplace and took the poker to it in order to help the wood catch.

"He truly seems to like Windridge. He's slept through the night ever since our coming here," Jessica said.

"Well, he is a year old now," Kate reminded them.

"It's so hard to believe," Jessica said. "When I think we've been here at Windridge for almost four months, I can't imagine where the time has gone. It seems like just yesterday we were sitting down to our first breakfast together."

"It only seems that way because you've hardly spoken two words to Devon since then," Kate admonished.

Buck chuckled but knew better than to join in the conversation. He quickly exited the room after replacing the poker against the wall. Kate watched him leave before turning her attention back to Jessica.

"You really should work out your differences."

"He wants to run my life — and Ryan's."

"He just cares about you and the boy.

He's good with Ryan, and Ryan really seems to love being with Devon. Why would you deprive the child of such a meaningful relationship? Devon's a good man."

"Yes, I suppose he is, but I cannot have Ryan getting close to someone who may well be gone tomorrow."

"Why would Devon be gone tomorrow? He loves Windridge — loves it as his own."

"But it isn't his. It's mine!" Jessica protested, knowing she sounded like a spoiled child arguing over toys. "Devon has interfered in my son's life, and he tries to manipulate and run mine. He tells me constantly how bad the finances are, but he never has suggestions as to how we could improve things. In fact, I'll bet he'd even laugh at our idea to sell quilts back East."

Kate smiled. "I kind of laughed at that idea myself, so don't hold that against Devon."

Jessica put her sewing aside and went to the fire. The warmth felt good to her. "I don't want to hold anything against anyone, Kate. I just want to be given due respect. I want Devon to realize that I love this place, too, and just because I didn't get a chance to grow up here doesn't mean I don't have Windridge's best interests in mind."

"So tell him that," Katie urged. "He's a

reasonable man. He'll listen."

Jessica shook her head. "But what if he doesn't? What if he just wants to fight with me?"

Kate laughed. "What if you step out the door and the lion eats you?"

"What?"

"It's in the Bible. The foolish man refuses to go about his duty because he's afraid if he steps out of the house, a lion might eat him. There's a lot of things in life like that. We refuse to take steps forward because we're afraid something overwhelming will happen."

Jessica nodded. "I just don't know how to take that man. He's so, well, he's too confident of himself. He acts like he has all the answers, and nobody else can possibly have anything good to say."

Kate shook her head. "I've never known Devon to fit that description. He's confident — that much I'll give you. But honestly, Jessica, his confidence is in the Lord rather than himself."

The muffled sound of Ryan's cry came from upstairs. Jessica immediately went to the sitting room door and pulled it open. "I think someone is telling us his naptime is over."

"I think you are right," Kate laughed. "It's

time for me to be putting supper together anyway. Those men are going to be hungry pretty soon, and I'm starting to feel a mite caved in myself."

Jessica, too, felt a slight gnawing of hunger. "What are we having tonight?"

"Roast," Kate replied. "Left over from last night, but tonight I'll fix it up in a stew with biscuits."

"Sounds wonderful."

With that, Jessica made her way upstairs. She had nearly reached the nursery door when Ryan's cries abated, and she could hear the sound of a male voice from within. She paused outside the door, wondering if Buck had gone to check the fire and had accidentally awakened the boy.

"There now, partner," came Devon's voice. "No sense in getting yourself all worked up. Ain't much good can come of it."

Jessica could hear Ryan's animated babble, as well as Devon moving around the room.

"Let's get you out of those wet clothes and into something more comfortable."

At this, Jessica could no longer stand idle. She burst through the door as though the house were on fire and stared daggers at Devon Carter. Her mind was flooded with thoughts of Essie Kappin trying to steal her son's loyalty by always insisting Jessica allow her to deal with the child whenever they were at the Kappins' for a visit.

"Just what do you think you're doing?" she protested. She came forward, grabbed Ryan out of Devon's arms, and maneuvered past him to the changing table. "Whatever possessed you to just allow yourself entry into my son's room?"

Ryan began to cry again, reaching around Jessica's tight hold toward where Devon stood rather stunned. Jessica hated that he was making such a scene. It was almost as if she were the monster having ripped him from the security of his parent, rather than the other way around.

"He was crying," Devon replied. "I figured he needed attention, and I was free for the moment."

Jessica plopped Ryan down on the changing table and set her mind on the job at hand rather than arguing with Devon. As soon as Ryan was changed and happily occupied on the rag rug with a toy, Jessica turned her full fury on Devon.

"I've told you before that I don't like having you interfere with my son."

Devon put his hands on his hips. His thick mustache twitched a bit as he frowned. "Jessica, this is a pretty isolated place. Don't you think we could agree to a truce of some sort?"

"No, I don't. I'm tired of telling you how I feel, only to have you ignore me." She hadn't noticed Ryan getting to his feet or the fact that he was walking, until he padded across the floor to Devon and took hold of his leg.

"Say, you did a right good job of that, little fellow," Devon said, clapping his hands.

Ryan laughed and let go to clap his own hands, only to smack down on his bottom. For a moment he looked startled, then he laughed again and got on his hands and knees as if to try the whole thing again.

Jessica, stunned that her son was walking, refused to allow him to make Devon the center of his attention. Devon was stealing her son away from her, and she could never allow that.

"If you don't mind," she said, snatching Ryan up protectively, "I'm needed downstairs to help with supper."

"I could watch him for you," Devon suggested.

Jessica could hardly believe he'd made the offer. He wasn't listening to her protests at all. Battling Ryan's squirming body, Jessica answered him as coolly as she dared. "You were hired to work the ranch, Mr. Carter, not the nursery." With that she left, refusing to give him a chance to reply. Oh, but the man could be infuriating.

Ryan began to cry, only furthering her frustration. One way or another, she would put an end to Devon's interference before he'd totally turned her son away from her. She would not have another situation on her hands where someone suggested her son was better off without her.

CHAPTER 4

Jessica spent the next two weeks feeling deeply convicted about her attitude and behavior toward Devon. Not only had he refused to share supper the night of their disagreement, but he had refused to share all subsequent meals from that night forward. Jessica knew the fault lay with her. She knew, too, that in order to deal with the matter and put things aright, she would have to be the one to do the apologizing.

She realized that Devon had meant only to be helpful, but her own insecurities regarding Ryan had caused her to act unforgivably bad. Sitting with her Bible in hand, Jessica felt hot tears trickle down her cheeks.

"I just don't want to lose Ryan's love, Lord," she whispered in the silence of her room. In the nursery Ryan already slept contentedly, but there would be no sleep for Jessica until she dealt with the matter at hand. Already she'd spent some fourteen restless nights, and her misery was rapidly catching up with her.

"I came here with such great expectations, Father," she began to pray again. "I thought there would be financial security and a place to belong. I have thought of the house on Windridge as my own special utopia since I was a small child. You know how I felt about it. You know I loved this place and always desired to be here. I just wanted everything to be perfect. I want to be perfect. The perfect mother. The perfect mistress of Windridge. But I fail and continue to fail no matter how hard I try."

She opened the Bible and found herself in the book of Colossians. " 'Put on therefore, as the elect of God, holy and beloved, bowels of mercies, kindness, humbleness of mind, meekness, longsuffering,' " she read aloud. Glancing past the desk where her Bible lay, Jessica peered out into the darkness of the night. Only the shadowy glow of lamplight from the cottage where Devon stayed could be seen on this moonless night.

"I certainly haven't been merciful or kind where he is concerned. Neither have I been meek or longsuffering, and I come nowhere near to being humble of mind. But Father, I'm so afraid. I'm afraid of failing once again. I failed Harriet when I pleaded to come west. I failed when I married Newman. I failed even when I was born — taking the life of my mother and the joy of my father. If I fail here, then what is left to me?

"If I fail to be a good mother to Ryan, then someone will come along and take him from me. And if I fail to bring this ranch back into prosperity, then I might well lose the roof over my head. I want to make things perfect, but I feel so inadequate. My life has been so far removed from perfection, and now that I finally have some say over it, nothing seems to be going right." She sighed and added with an upward glance, "What do I do?"

She felt the turmoil intensify and continued to read from Colossians. " 'Forbearing one another, and forgiving one another, if any man have a quarrel against any: even as Christ forgave you, so also do ye. And above all these things put on charity, which is the bond of perfectness.' "

Jessica returned her gaze to the cottage. *I've not been forbearing or forgiving, and I certainly haven't put on charity. I've shown Devon Carter nothing but anger and resentment.* She thought of the close, affectionate manner in which Devon handled Ryan, and her heart ached. The situation tested every emotion within her. On one hand she feared Devon's involvement because of the Kappins. And on the other hand she feared Ryan's reaction to Devon's attention.

She couldn't provide Ryan with a father. Certainly not a father like Devon. Was it fair or right to allow the boy to grow close to Devon, when the man could pick up and go at any given moment? Kate said Devon would never do such a thing, but what if he grew tired of the failing ranch? What if he left them like so many of the other ranch hands had already done?

"Oh Father, what am I to do? How do I show this man charity instead of fear?" Then a thought came to mind, causing Jessica to feel even more at a loss. Devon seemed perfectly willing to answer her questions, to take time out of his schedule to work with her on matters — at least those times when she had allowed herself to ask and seek his help. But the relaxed nature of Devon — his considerate and generous spirit — made Jessica uncomfortable. Devon clearly represented the kind of man she would have chosen for herself had others not interfered with her life.

"If Harriet hadn't thrust me into her social circles, demanding I choose a husband from the men of leisure who haunted

96

her doorstep, I might have known true happiness. I might even have come here and met Devon Carter long before joining my life to Newman; then Ryan would be his son, and I would be his wife."

The thought so startled Jessica that she slammed the Bible shut. *I can't allow myself to think that way,* she scolded. *There is nothing to be gained by it. I can't take back the past. I can't bring my dead mother and father to life and start over under their care instead of Aunt Harriet's. I can't remake my life.*

The light went out in the cottage, leaving Jessica to feel even more deserted. Somehow, knowing that Devon was awake made her feel less alone. As if taking this as her own cue to go to bed, Jessica made one more check on Ryan, then turned down the lamp and crawled into the massive bed. Scooting into the very middle, Jessica could extend both arms and never touch the sides of the bed. How empty it seemed. How empty her entire life seemed.

I'll try to do better, Lord, she prayed the promise. *I will humble myself and go to Devon and apologize for my attitude and actions. I will even be honest with him about the reasons. But please, just go before me and help me to say the right thing. Don't let me make a fool out of myself — again.*

■ ■ ■ ■

The next morning dawned with a promise of spring. The air felt warm on Jessica's face as she made her way out to what Kate called the garden house. The ground gave off a rich, earthy smell that made Jessica want to plant something. Maybe she'd talk to Kate about restoring the flower garden that used to grow along this walk. Kate had spoken of the prairie flowers and the delicate splotches of color that graced the hills when springtime was upon them in full. Kate said it had been Naomi's favorite time of year.

Standing just outside the cottage, Jessica gave a brief prayer for courage. She wanted to speak to Devon before breakfast in hopes that he might join them and ease the tension that had engulfed the house since Jessica's last outburst. She also intended to follow through with her promise to God and humble herself before this handsome stranger.

Knocking lightly, Jessica tried to plan what she'd say. She had continued to wrestle with her conscience long into the night, but somewhere around two in the morning, she'd finally let go of her fears and given them over to God. It wouldn't be easy to face her mismatched emotions, but somehow she knew God would give her the grace to handle things day by day.

Devon opened the door, stared at her blankly for a moment, then smiled. "And to what do I owe the pleasure of a visit from the boss lady?"

Jessica swallowed hard and tried to think of each word before speaking. "I've come here to apologize."

Devon crossed his arms and leaned against the door frame. "Apologize?"

Jessica nodded. "That's right. My behavior toward you has been uncalled for. I've known it all along, but I'm hoping you will give me a chance to explain."

Devon's expression softened. "Why don't you come in and tell me all about it."

Jessica nodded. "All right."

She entered the cottage for the first time, amazed at the hominess of the front room. A native stone fireplace took up most of one wall, while a big picture window that looked out onto a small porch graced yet another. A narrow pine staircase took up the south side, while an open archway made up most of the remaining west wall. A large rag rug, no doubt put together by Kate, lay on the floor in front of the fireplace, and a couch, upholstered in a sort of brown tweed, stood awaiting them behind this.

"Might as well sit over here," Devon said, leading the way to the couch. "It's really the only warm spot in the house. Buck and I are trying to find materials to make repairs, but it's rather slow going."

"If there's anything I can do to help . . . ," Jessica offered, letting her voice trail off.

"That's all right. I think Buck and I can handle it," Devon countered. "So you were going to do some explaining."

Jessica nodded. She gazed into Devon's dark eyes and felt a wave of alarm wash over her. Maybe coming here wasn't a good idea, after all. She looked away and clasped her fingers tightly together. "I know I've treated you rather harshly."

"Rather harshly?" he questioned.

Jessica took a deep breath and let it out. "All right. I've treated you badly, and I'm sorry. There's a great deal in my life that makes it hard for me to trust people. Especially strangers. From the minute I stepped foot on Windridge, you seemed to be everywhere, and frankly, it made me uncomfortable."

"I can certainly understand," Devon replied. "That's kind of why I've been trying to keep my distance."

"Then there's Ryan," she continued uneasily. Devon was a man. What would he understand of her motherly insecurities? She looked up and found his expression fixed with a compassionate stare. Maybe he would understand. "Do you know my story, Mr. Carter? How I came to live back East rather than on Windridge?" He nodded. "Well, it's left me with a very real void in my life. I never knew my parents — never saw my father until I was twelve. Even when I came here to spend a few weeks that summer, I still didn't see him much. He probably felt as uncomfortable as I did. Neither one of us knew what to do with the other one."

She paused as if trying to sort out her words. She wanted Devon to understand why she resented his interference with Ryan, but it seemed important to set up the conflicts from her early days in order to make her present days more clear.

"I never felt love for my father," she admitted. "I think I was afraid to love him. I certainly didn't want to give him another chance to send me away or to reject that love. My aunt Harriet encouraged neither shows of emotion nor words of endearment, and so I never felt loved in her home. I've been taught most of my life to bury my emotions, or at best, to shut them off. I tell you this because I would like for you to understand my difficulty in being open with my feelings."

Devon chuckled. "I thought you made your feelings quite apparent. You don't like me or my interfering with Ryan."

"No, that's not it," Jessica replied, looking at the dying embers in the fireplace. "I love Windridge. It's the only thing that couldn't reject my love." Her voice trembled slightly under the emotion of the moment. "I don't want my pride to keep this ranch from becoming a success once again. I don't want my feelings from the past creeping into the future of this place, and I won't allow myself to cause the demise of Buck and Kate's happiness, nor of yours."

"You don't have the power to put an end to Buck and Kate's happiness. Nor can you destroy mine for that matter," Devon replied, seeming most emphatic. "As for the success of this ranch, well, maybe the time has come to put an end to Windridge. There are folks out there willing to buy. Maybe you'd be happier back East or even in town."

"No!" Jessica said, looking back to see Devon watching her reaction with apparent interest. "I don't want to sell. If I gave you that idea, then I know I've failed to say the right words. Look, I mentioned the idea of a resort ranch only because it seemed to be profitable. We're only an hour away from the train. We already have a perfectly suited stagecoach, though why my father ever purchased such an elaborate means of transportation, I'll never know."

Devon laughed. "Gus got it in trade, to tell you the truth. One of the locals ran a stage line for about two months. He went broke in a hurry and then took sick. When he saw he couldn't keep it up, he asked Gus to trade him for some good beef stock so his son could start a small ranch. Gus agreed, and there you have it."

"Well, that does explain it rather neatly," Jessica agreed. "But don't you see? I envision the healing power of this ranch will draw others to its doorstep, just as it has me."

"But honestly, Jessica," he said, his voice lowering and his expression growing intense, "part of Windridge's healing is the isolation. You bring in a bunch of city folks and suddenly it's not so very isolated anymore. Folks will come with their strange notions and ways of doing things, and soon you'll find that Windridge is nothing like it once was. I'd hate to see that happen."

Jessica felt a bit defeated. She honestly

tried to see Devon's point. Maybe he knew what he was talking about. Maybe she was the real fool in the matter. She reached into her apron pocket and pulled out several folded pieces of paper. "These are the articles I mentioned to you awhile back. All I ask is that you take a look at them."

Devon reached out to take them, his fingers closing over hers for a brief moment. The current of emotions seemed to leap from Jessica to Devon, and for a time he looked at her as if he could read every detail of her soul. The longing, the loneliness, the fearfulness, and the insecurity — Jessica worried that if she didn't look away quickly, she'd soon reveal more about herself than she'd ever intended. She dropped her hold on the papers and pulled her hand back against her breast as though the touch had burned her fingers.

Devon seemed to understand her discomfort, but to what extent, Jessica couldn't tell. "I'll look these over," he promised, tucking them between the cushions of the couch.

"I appreciate that. I also have another favor to ask you."

"All right."

She lowered her head and stared at her lap. "I would very much appreciate your help with the Windridge accounts. I've looked at the books, but I'm still not sure what I'm looking at."

Devon chuckled. "I can't say that Gus was the best bookkeeper in the world. He knew his system but seldom wanted to share it with anyone else. It wasn't until about a year before he died that I knew we were in real trouble. After that, things just sort of went from bad to worse. But in answer to your question, I'll be glad to do what I can. I do know the workings of this ranch — very nearly as well as Buck. I think together we can give some strong consideration as to what is to be done."

Jessica nodded. "Thank you. I do appreciate it. I know I've not acted with Christian charity, and God has quite seriously brought it to my attention." She glanced up to find him studying her. Her heart skipped a beat when he grinned at her.

"He's had to bring it to my attention quite often as well — not because of your attitude," he said, pausing, "but because of my own."

Jessica got to her feet. The intimacy of the moment was rapidly becoming quite noticeable. "I hope this apology of mine will mean that you'll reconsider and share meals up at the house again. Kate hasn't been herself since you stopped coming up, and I know you're staying away because of the way I acted."

Devon walked with her to the door. "That's not exactly true," he told her. "I also stayed away because of the way I acted when I was around you."

Jessica turned to look at him — wondering at his meaning — afraid to know the truth. Instead of asking him to explain, she realized she'd omitted a very important matter. "There's one more thing, and it comes very hard for me."

"By all means, speak your mind."

Jessica looked at him for a moment. She felt down deep inside that she could trust this man. That his motives were pure and his actions were not intended for harm. What she wasn't sure of was whether or not she could accept that her child would have needs in his life that she would be unable to fill — needs that would require a man's thought, perspective, and guidance.

"It's about Ryan," she finally said.

"I see."

Devon took a step back and looked like he might say something, but Jessica hurried to continue. "I was wrong there as well." He raised a brow but said nothing, and Jessica realized she'd have to explain further. But how much should she say? Would it be appropriate to tell Devon about Esmerelda and her mother? Would it be appropriate to explain her deepest heartfelt fear that she might somehow lose Ryan to another?

She looked away, tears forming in her eyes. How could she explain? She scarcely understood the feelings she had. She felt so protective of Ryan, not only for him, but for fear she would once again be denied love.

"I'm sorry," she whispered. "It's very difficult for me to speak about it."

Devon's voice was low and filled with tenderness. "Jessica, I know you're still grieving your husband's passing and all. I wasn't trying to take his place."

Jessica laughed and turned to meet Devon with her tears flowing freely. "It isn't that. Believe me, it isn't that at all." Her voice sounded foreign in her own ears. It came out as a mixture of a laugh and a sob all at once. "I didn't love Newman Albright, and he certainly didn't love me. We married because he was chosen by my aunt Harriet. I often thought afterwards that for all she did to sing his charms and merits, Harriet should have married him herself."

Devon reached out and touched her tear-streaked cheek. "Then what is this all about?"

"I might never have loved my husband,

but I would die rather than lose my son," she answered, quivering under the touch of his warm fingers.

"I still don't understand what that has to do with me."

He looked at her with such intensity, such longing to understand, that Jessica had to close her eyes to regain her composure. "The only reason," she began, her eyes still tightly closed, "that I didn't want you interfering with Ryan —"

"Yes? Go on," he encouraged when she fell silent.

"I don't want you replacing me in his life," she finally managed, but the tears came again. "He's all I have." Her voice came out like a whimper, and Jessica hated sounding like a lost child. She knew it was better to be honest and face humiliation than to lie and go on dealing with her conscience.

To her surprise, Devon put his arms around her and gently pulled her head to his shoulder. No one had ever done this for her. Not once. Not even Newman. The action seemed so intimate, so loving, that Jessica broke down and cried in deep, heart-wrenching sobs.

Devon did nothing but hold her. He let her cry, all the time keeping his arms tightly around her. He didn't say a word or try to force answers out of her. He just held her. Oh, but it felt wonderful! It felt like something Jessica had been searching for all of her life. Warm arms to comfort and assure her that the world outside would not break in to hurt her anymore. Without even realizing it, she had wrapped her own arms around Devon's waist and clung to him as though in letting go, she might well drown in a sea of emptiness.

After a few minutes, Jessica felt the weight of her emotions lift. Her tears subsided, and she fell silent. She knew it was quite uncalled for to be standing there alone with Devon, embracing him so familiarly, but she was quite hesitant to let go.

"Feel better?" he asked softly, reaching a hand up to smooth back her hair.

Jessica sniffed in a most unladylike way and nodded. "I think so." She let go of him and wiped her face with the edge of her apron. "I'm sorry about losing control that way."

"Don't be," Devon answered quite seriously. "You don't have to face the world by yourself, Jess."

The nickname warmed her, where only weeks ago it would have irritated her. "I know. I know. The Bible makes that clear, but sometimes it seems God is so far away."

"I wasn't talking about God." She looked up to see Devon's eyes narrow ever so slightly as he scrutinized her. "God is there for you," he agreed. "I wouldn't presume to say otherwise. But I meant that we're here for you, too. Katie, Buck, and me. We care about you, and we care about Ryan. And honestly, Jessica, I would never do anything to harm your child or to take him away from you. I do realize that there is more to this than you're telling me, but maybe one day you'll feel confident enough of our friendship to share it all. Until then, just know I care.

"We'll get through this, but we'll need to rely on one another. Ryan is starting to walk now, and there are plenty of dangers around the ranch. You'll wear yourself to the bone if you worry about having to watch him alone. Let us help you. We want to make your life easier, not harder, and certainly not more painful."

Jessica nodded. "I know that." She lowered her head and looked at the floor. What she would say next would come at considerable risk to her security. "Ryan seems so miserable without you around. I want you to feel free to play with him and be around him. I know he's already taken to you in a big way.

I would even go so far as to say he loves you."

Devon reached out to touch Jessica's chin with his index finger. Lifting her face, he replied, "He loves you, too, Jessica. That won't change just because other people come into his life. It's been my experience, the more love the better. People need to be loved."

Jessica felt his words cut deep into her heart. If she didn't clear out now, she'd start crying all over again. "Thank you," she whispered quickly and hurried to the door. Throwing it open, she looked back over her shoulder. "I'm sure Kate has breakfast nearly ready. You will join us, won't you?"

"You bet. I'll be up to the house in a few minutes."

Devon watched Jessica walk up the path to the big stone house. He felt an overwhelming urge to run after her and declare his love for her. Funny, he thought, he'd fallen in love with her almost from the start. At least he thought it was love. He certainly knew that it was something powerful and strong. He thought about her constantly and worried that she would give up on the ranch before he had a chance to convince her to take his help.

He had money in the bank. Not a lot, but enough to help the ranch. He would just do as Buck and Kate had done and start purchasing things as they needed them, and he wouldn't let Jessica know about it. Of course, Buck would know, and so would Kate. But he knew they would keep his secret. Kate had told him of their scheme to sell quilts. Maybe he'd offer to take some to Kansas City when he went there to buy cattle. He could always add some extra dollars to the amount he actually managed to make.

It was easy enough to formulate an idea about bringing in more cattle and maybe a ranch hand or two, but it was harder to decide how he would help Jessica to work through her inability to trust. He longed to help her feel secure in the house on Windridge. He wanted her to know that her home would be here as long as she needed it. That he would be here, too, if only she would let him.

He thought of her fears of losing Ryan's love and realized rather quickly that with Jessica's very personal declarations of her life, he had become privy to the knowledge that she had never felt loved. Kate had loved her from the start and had said so on many occasions. But Kate had not been allowed to raise the baby of Naomi and Gus Gussop. A cold, unfeeling woman with social concerns had raised Jessica. The father Jessica had never known had no idea how to receive her or her needs when that unfeeling woman had finally allowed Jessica a visit home.

Even her husband hadn't married her out of love. And Devon found that particularly distressing considering his own growing feelings. He hadn't said anything about his interest in Jessica, primarily because he assumed she wouldn't be ready for such attentions. Now he realized she was not only ready for it, but she'd been ready for over twenty-seven years. She needed love. She needed the love of a good man.

He smiled and leaned against the doorjamb as Jessica disappeared through the back door of the house. "I'm a good man," he said aloud, a plan already formulating in his mind. His smile broadened. "In fact, I'm the only man for the job."

He looked up into the clear morning sky and felt the overwhelming urge to share his thoughts with God. "This was what You had in mind for me all along, wasn't it? I wouldn't have been happy with another woman, and that's why You didn't let me waste my life on Jane Jenkins."

He thought of the petite blond who'd appeared at the ranch less than two weeks before their wedding day to announce she was marrying someone else. At least she'd been good enough to bring back Devon's ring. The ring had belonged to his grandmother, and Jane knew how much it meant to him. She hadn't been totally without feeling.

"I can't stay out here in the middle of nowhere," she had told him that day so long ago. *"I hate Kansas and everything that goes with it. I want to see the world and live in a big city, and I've found someone who feels exactly like I do. I hope you'll forgive me like you said you would."*

Last Devon had heard, Jane was living just outside of Topeka. She had three kids, a cantankerous mother-in-law, and a husband who was seldom home due to his job as a traveling salesman. He felt sorry for her, knowing her dream had not been realized. At the time, her rejection had hurt him deeply; but as the months and years passed, Devon knew God had saved him from a miserable life.

"Thank You," he whispered. "Thank You for sending Jane out of my life and for bringing Jessica into it. Now, it's my prayer that You would show me how to help her.

How to make her feel loved and safe."

He realized they would all be sitting down to breakfast soon, so he grabbed his hat and closed the door to the cottage. "It wouldn't hurt if You helped her to love me, too." He grinned and tapped his hat onto his head. "Wouldn't hurt at all."

CHAPTER 5

One of Jessica's greatest pleasures came from horseback riding. Buck had suggested it one glorious April day, and Jessica found it a perfect solution to those times when the house seemed too quiet and the day too long. Of course, with Ryan now getting into things, those times were few and far between, but nevertheless, Jessica found it a wonderful time. Riding out across the prairie hills, she could think about the days to come — and the days now gone. She could plan her future without anyone barging in on her thoughts, and she could pray.

It also became an exercise in trust. She forced herself to leave Ryan in Kate's care and trust that nothing would happen to threaten her relationship with her son. It wasn't easy, but Jessica knew instinctively that it was right.

Now, having ridden to the top of the ridge, Jessica stared out across the rolling

Flint Hills and sighed. Flowers were just beginning to dot the prairie grasses. It reminded her of her mother. Kate had told her that this view had been Naomi's favorite because of the flowers and the contours of the hills and the glorious way the sunsets seemed to spill color across the western horizon.

Jessica wearied of the saddle and dismounted. "All right, boy, it's back to the barn for you."

The horse seemed to perfectly understand her, and with a snort and a whinny, he took off in the direction of the corrals and barn. By letting the horse go free, she found that he always made his way back to the stable and to Buck's tender care. The first time it had happened totally by mistake when Jessica had dismounted and let go of her reins. Buck had worried she'd been thrown, but Jessica had assured him as she came running down the hill to recapture her mount that she was fine. Buck had laughed; so had Devon; and when they'd shared the scene with Katie, she had laughed as well. Buck said the Windridge horses were so spoiled and pampered, they'd return to the barn every time, and after that, it just became the routine.

Today, the wind came from the south as it

often did, but with it came a gentle scent of new life. Flowers bloomed sporadically across the prairie, and Jessica reveled in the addition of color to her otherwise rather drab world. The fields had greened up, much to the delight of the cattle who seemed rather tired of hay and dried dead grass. Even the house itself seemed to take on a more golden hue.

Jessica sighed and reached up to take off her bonnet. She let down her hair and shook it free, grateful to feel the wind through it one more time. Kate said her father had called this God's country, and Jessica could well understand why he felt that way. Just standing there, watching the cattle feed, seeing the occasional movement of a rabbit or the flight of birds overhead, Jessica felt her heart overflow with praise to God. His presence seemed to be everywhere at once.

The land was so wholly unspoiled. The city had a harshness to it that she'd once accused the prairie of having. Both could be ruthless in dealing with their tenants, but while the prairie did so from innocence, the city made its mark in snobbery, class strife, and confrontation.

In the city, Jessica seldom knew a moment when noise didn't dominate her day. The activities were enough to cause a person to go mad. And it seemed the poorer you were, the higher the level of clatter. Street vendors called out their wares from morning to night. Children — dirty urchins who had no real homes — raced up and down the streets begging money, food, shelter. Poverty brought its own sounds: the cries of the hungry, the street fighting of the angry, the con men with their schemes to make everyone rich overnight.

But always the needs of the children concerned Jessica. She had tried to do what she could, but there'd been so little, and she could hardly take away from her own child in order to provide for someone else's. When her father had started to provide for her once again, she had shared what she could with some of the others. Esmerelda had thought her quite mad. "Charity," she had told Jessica, "is better left to the truly rich." Essie thought Jessica's money could be much better spent on a new gown or toys for Ryan. It was easy now to see how harsh Essie could be when Jessica refused to play by her rules.

And there were so many rules. Not just Essie's but New York's rules as well. The rules of class — of not crossing boundaries, of staying where you belonged. Jessica had provided a dichotomy for her friends. She had been raised in the best social settings with Harriet Nelson and married a man who held rank among the well-to-do. But when their money was gone, so, too, were their friends. It seemed strange to suddenly find that she was never invited to parties or teas. Never visited by those she had once been bosom companions with. Essie had maintained a letter-writing campaign, but never once had the young woman come to visit after things had gone bad for Jessica. She hadn't even come to Newman's funeral.

But once Jessica's father stepped in to move her back to the proper neighborhood and reinstate her with financial resources, everyone flocked around. It was all as if Jessica had only been abroad for several years. In fact, Essie had once introduced her that way, telling the dinner guests that Jessica had enjoyed an extensive stay in Paris. It was true enough that she had done exactly that, but Essie failed to mention that Jessica had been thirteen years old at the time.

She let her gaze pan across the western horizon, while the waning sun touched her face with the slightest hint of warmth. She knew Aunt Harriet would have been appalled to find her in such a state, but to Jessica, it felt wonderful! She cherished the moment, just as she had when she'd been twelve.

"Thank You, Father," she whispered, raising her hands heavenward as if to stretch out and touch her fingertips to God.

"You make a mighty fetching picture up here like that," Devon said.

Jessica turned, surprised to see the overworked foreman making his way up the ridge. "I thought maybe you'd hightailed it back to civilization," she teased to ease her own embarrassment. "I've scarcely seen you in two weeks."

"There's been too much to do," Devon told her. "But you already know that. Kate told me you've been pretty busy yourself."

"Yes. We've finished up some quilts, and then Buck dug us up a garden patch."

"I saw that. Can't say this is good farm ground, but Kate's gardens generally survive. It's all that tender loving care she gives them." Devon took off his hat and wiped his brow with a handkerchief. "Feels good up here."

"Yes," Jessica agreed. Her hair whipped wildly in the breeze, and she felt a bit embarrassed to be found in such a state. It was one thing to know they could see her from down below the hilltop, but for Devon to be here with her made Jessica self-conscious.

She reached up and began trying to pull her hair back into order, but Devon came forward and stilled her efforts. "Don't do that. It looks so nice down."

Jessica laughed nervously and stepped away. "It's just something I do sometimes. Kind of silly, but it reminds me of when I was a little girl."

"Nothing silly about that."

"Maybe not," Jessica said, forcing herself to look away from Devon's attractive face to the start of a beautiful sunset. "The prairie used to make me lonely. I used to feel so small and insignificant in the middle of it all. The hills just go on and on forever. It reminds me of how I'm just one tiny speck in a very big world."

"What happened to change how you felt? I mean, you told me you wanted to stay here and never leave. Surely you wouldn't feel that way about a place that made you feel lonely and insignificant."

Devon had come to stand beside her again, but Jessica refused to look at him. "I never had many chances to visit here before getting married, but after the second visit, I had already decided that the prairie was growing on me. I went home to New York City and felt swallowed up whole. The lifestyle, the parties, the activities that never seemed to end — it all made me feel so forgotten."

"How so?" Devon questioned softly.

Jessica stopped toying with her hair and let it go free once again. "No one really ever talks to anyone there. You speak about the city, about the affairs of other people. You talk about the newest rages and the fashionable way to dress. You go to parties and dinners and present yourself to be seen with all the correct people, but you never, ever tell anyone how you feel about anything personal. It fit well with my upbringing, but I came to want more."

She finally looked at him. "I feel alive out here. I feel like I can breathe and stretch and let my hair blow in the wind and no one will rebuke me for it. I feel like I can talk to you and Buck and Kate, and you not only talk back, but you really listen."

"I can't imagine being any other way," Devon said. "But, as for the coldness of the big city, I do understand. I go to Kansas City once, sometimes twice a year for supplies and to sell off the cattle. I hate it there. No one seems to care if you live or die."

"I know," Jessica replied, admiring the way the sky had taken on a blend of orange, yellow, and pink. "And you certainly never get sunsets like these."

Devon laughed. "Nope."

"I know God brought me here for a reason. I know He has a purpose for my life, and I feel strongly that my purpose involves helping other people. That may sound silly to you, but I know God has a plan for me."

"It doesn't sound silly at all. I believe God has a plan for each of us."

"What kind of plan does He have for you, Devon?" she asked seriously, concentrating on his expression.

Devon shoved his hands into his pockets and stared to the west. "I don't guess I know in full."

"So tell me in part," she urged.

"I know God brought me to this ranch. It was a healing for me, so when you speak of it being a healing for other people, I guess I understand. I was once engaged to be married, but it didn't work out. Windridge saw me through some bad times. Now, however, I feel God has shown me the reason for that situation and the result."

"What reason?" Jessica questioned, truly wondering how Devon could speak so casually about losing the woman he apparently loved.

"I know God has someone else for me to

marry. He's already picked her out."

"Oh," she replied, her answer sounding flat. She'd only recently allowed herself to think about Devon as something more than a ranch foreman. She'd actually given herself permission to consider what it might be like to fall in love and marry a man like Devon Carter. His words came as a shock and stung her effectively into silence.

"I don't like being alone. I see myself with a family of my own. Six or seven — boys, girls, it doesn't matter — and a fine spread to work. Ranches can be excellent places to bring up children."

He looked at her as if expecting her to comment, but Jessica had no idea what to say. His words only told her that one day he would go his way and leave her alone. Not only that but leave Ryan alone as well. A dull ache caused her to abruptly change the subject.

"I see Windridge surviving and becoming stronger. I think we have a lot to offer folks here. Have you had a chance to look over those articles I left with you?"

"I've looked them over. I have to say I'm not nearly as against the idea as I once was. It seems the ranch would mostly be open to the public during summer months, is that right?"

Jessica perked up at his positive attitude. "Yes. Yes, that's right. Late spring to early autumn might be the biggest stretch of time, but basically it would be summer."

"Ranches can be mighty busy during the summer," he commented.

"Yes, but that's part of the attraction. Folks from back East will come to see the workings of the ranch. You and your men would be able to go about your business, and the visitors would be able to observe you in action."

"They'd also want to ride and maybe even try their hand at what we do, at least that's what one of your clippings said," Devon countered.

"But only if we wanted it to be that way," Jessica replied. "It can be arranged however we see fit. No one makes the rules but us."

"I suppose it wouldn't be so bad if the rest of the year allowed us to get back to normal. The location does seem right for something like that. I suppose we could even fix one of the larger ponds with a deck and a place for fishing."

"What a good idea," Jessica replied. "Maybe swimming, too."

Devon nodded. "Hmmm, maybe. Might be a bit cold. Remember, those aren't hot springs." He appeared to be genuinely considering the matter. "And you see this as a ministry?"

Jessica felt herself grow slightly defensive. "I do. I see a great many things we can share with people. Kindness and love, mercy, tolerance — you name it. I know it would be a resort, and people would pay to come here and rest, but how we handled their stay would be evidence of Christ working in our lives. They would see how we dealt with problems and handled our daily lives."

"One of the articles talked about taking folks out camping under the stars to give them a taste of what the pioneers experienced when they went west in covered wagons. You thinking about doing that?" Devon asked.

Jessica considered the matter for a moment. "I think at first it would be to our benefit to just keep small. We could advertise it very nearly like a boarding home for vacationers. We could offer quiet summers. Maybe fishing, like you suggested, and horseback riding. We could build some nice chairs for the porch, and Kate and I could make cushions; folks could go through my father's library and pick out something to read and just relax on the porch. I just want to make a difference in people's lives."

Devon stepped closer. "You've made a difference in mine. You and Ryan both."

She looked into his warm brown eyes and saw a reflection of something she didn't understand. His words sounded important, yet he'd made it clear that God had someone already in mind for him to marry.

"I need to get back." She turned to leave, but Devon reached out to touch her arm. "I meant it, Jess. And I'm starting to think that maybe a resort wouldn't be a bad way to get the ranch back up and running. Hopefully, this small herd we've taken on from the Rocking W will make us a tidy profit and allow us to get a bigger herd next year. You keep praying about it, and so will I."

Jessica nodded and hurried down the hill to the three-story stone house. She didn't know how to take Devon or his words. He always treated her kindly and always offered her honesty, but today only served to confuse her.

Quietly, she entered the house through the back door, hoping that she'd not have to deal with Kate. Kate would want to know how Jessica had spent her day. Kate would want to know what she and Devon had talked about. And there was little doubt in Jessica's mind that Kate would know they had talked. She'd probably observed them up on the ridge. Everyone would have seen them there. Buck. The ranch hands.

Jessica felt her face grow hot. She had very much enjoyed being with Devon, and she enjoyed their talks. But Devon had another woman in mind to marry, and Jessica knew the heartache of losing a man to another woman. She'd not interfere in Devon's relationships. She'd not ruin his chances at happiness with the woman of his dreams. The woman God had sent to him.

With a heavy heart, Jessica admitted to herself that she was gradually coming to care about Devon. She liked the way he moved, the way he talked. She loved how he played with Ryan and how Ryan's face lit up whenever Devon came into the room. Reluctantly, Jessica began to put her hair back up in a bun. "I'm being so childish and ridiculous," she muttered.

"Oh, so there you are. Guess who just woke up?" Kate asked, coming down the back stairs with Ryan in her arms.

Jessica had just secured the last hairpin in place. "How's Mama's boy?" Jessica asked, holding her arms out to Ryan.

"Mamamama," Ryan chattered. "Eat." He pulled at Jessica's collar, and she knew he wanted to nurse. She'd only managed to wean him a couple weeks earlier, but he nevertheless tried to coerce her into nursing him.

"Mama will take you to the kitchen and get you a big boy's cup," Jessica told him, gently tousling his nearly hairless head. "Do you suppose this child will ever grow hair?" she asked Kate.

"I've heard it said you were the same way," Kate said chuckling. "I think you finally achieved those glossy brown curls when you were nearly two."

"I hope he doesn't take too long," Jessica replied as she retraced her steps to the kitchen. She thought for a moment she was off the hook until Kate, pouring fresh cold milk into a cup for Ryan, asked, "So what did you and Devon have to talk about while you enjoyed that beautiful sunset?"

Jessica tried not to act in the leastwise concerned about the question. "We discussed the ranch. It consumes most of our talks. Devon is finally coming around to my way of thinking. He's not nearly so negative about turning this place into a resort ranch."

"I never thought you'd convince him, but he talked to Buck about it just yesterday. Buck said he actually had some good ideas about what they could do to make this place ready by next year."

"Next year? But Devon said nothing to

me about next year. I figured I'd have to spend most of this one just convincing him to let me do it."

Ryan drank from the cup, finished the milk, then tried to pound the empty cup against the wall behind his mother. Jessica finally put him down on the floor and turned her attention back to Kate.

"Did he really say next summer?"

Kate smiled and pushed up her glasses. "He did. I take it that surprises you?"

"Indeed it does. He said only that he was starting to see some merit in the idea. I had no idea he was actually working toward a date."

"Well, he's found some extra capital to sink into the ranch. Then, too, we have the quilts to sell, and we can always busy ourselves to make more. Besides, Devon doesn't own this ranch — you do. If you want to turn it into a resort, you certainly don't need anyone's permission."

"Yes, but I want you all to be happy."

"Devon, too?" Kate grinned.

"Of course. You told me I needed to consider his thoughts on the matter, and I have. I respect Devon's opinion. I know all of you understand the ranch better than I do, but nevertheless, I want to learn, and I want to keep everyone's best interests at heart. I've been praying hard about this, Kate. I'm not going to just jump in without thinking."

Kate reached out and gave Jessica a hug. "I knew you wouldn't. We want you happy though, and if turning this place upside down would do the trick, I have a feeling Devon would start working on plans to figure a way."

Jessica said nothing but turned instead to see Ryan heading for the stove. "No, Ryan! Hot!" she exclaimed and went quickly to move the boy to another part of the kitchen.

"Why don't you and Ryan go out on the porch and spend some time together?" Kate suggested. "I've already got supper well underway, and there's no need to have you both in here underfoot."

Jessica laughed. "Just when I started thinking I had become needed and useful."

Kate laughed. "Oh, you're needed and useful, all right. Maybe more than you realize."

Jessica picked up the boy and made her way to the front door and out onto the porch. The sky had turned deep lavender with hints of even darker blues to the east. Night was still another hour or so away, but already shadows fell across the hills and valleys. Jessica liked the effect and wished fervently she could draw or paint. It seemed a shame that something so lovely should go by unseen. This thought provoked another. She could always advertise the ranch to artists. Mention the beautiful scenery and lighting. Of course, many people would consider the scenery boring and anything but beautiful. Perhaps that wouldn't be a very productive thing to do. What if someone went home to complain about the falsehood of her advertisement?

As Ryan played happily with Katie's flowerpots, Jessica allowed her thoughts to go back to Devon. She couldn't help it. She didn't want to care about him, at least not in the sense of falling in love and sharing a life with him. She didn't like to think of the rejection that could come in caring for someone, only to have them not care in return.

Still, if she couldn't have him in that capacity, then it was enough to have him here on the ranch full time. He made a good foreman, and she prayed he'd stay on for as long as she kept the ranch. A gray cloud descended over her thoughts. What if he married and brought his wife here to Windridge? Jessica shuddered. She'd not like that at all. And then with Ryan already so attached to Devon, it might create even greater problems. What if Ryan wanted to be with Devon instead of Jessica? What if Devon's new wife attracted Ryan's attention as well?

Jessica shook off the thoughts and tried to remain positive. "I can't be given over to thoughts of what if. There's plenty of other things to worry myself with."

Ryan babbled on and on about the flowerpots. Some words came out in clarity, and others were purely baby talk. Jessica found herself amazed to see how much the child had grown over the last few weeks. It seemed he'd almost aged overnight. She didn't like to think of him growing up and not needing her anymore. She didn't like to think about him becoming an adult and moving away. What would she do when he was gone? Who would love her, and whom would she love?

Devon's image came to mind, but Jessica shook her head sadly. "That's not going to happen," she told herself again. "He has other plans, and they don't include me."

Ryan perked up at this and toddled back to Jessica. He pounded the flats of his hands on her knees. "Me. Me. Me go. Me go."

Jessica looked down at him, feeling tears form in her eyes. "I know you will," she told him sadly. "One day, you will go."

CHAPTER 6

"If we convert those two sitting rooms at the back of the house," Kate said one evening after dinner, "we could have additional bedrooms for guests."

"True," Buck replied, looking to Jessica and Devon for their reactions.

"It might even work better if Ryan and I took those two rooms and let our rooms upstairs be used for guests," Jessica replied. "I mean, that way the entire second floor would be devoted to guests, and the third floor would still belong to you and Buck."

"Maybe it would be better to give the third floor to you and Ryan," Devon said thoughtfully. "After all, Kate needs to be close to the kitchen to get things started up in the morning, and Buck needs to be close to the barn and bunkhouse."

"I hadn't thought of it that way," Kate replied. "Those two rooms would be more than enough for Buck and me. In fact, one room would be enough."

"No, now I wouldn't feel right about it if you and Buck didn't have your own sitting room for privacy," Jessica said firmly. "Having a house full of strangers will be cause enough to need our own places of refuge."

"I could give you back the cottage," Devon offered. "If you and Buck think you'd be more comfortable there, I could move into the bunkhouse."

"Nonsense," Kate said shaking her head. "You've already moved once; you might as well stay put." Jessica wondered what she meant by this statement, but the conversation moved along so quickly that she never had a chance to ask.

"Katie and I would be happy just about any place you put us," Buck stated. "I think those two sitting rooms are just perfect for us. It would eliminate running up and down all those stairs, and what with my rheumatism acting up from time to time, that would be enough to motivate the move on my part."

"Buck, you should have told me you were having trouble," Jessica countered. "I would have seen to it that you and Kate were moved long ago had I known."

"The exercise does us good," Kate said. "But I agree with Buck and Devon. Moving us downstairs into those back rooms would be perfect. That way, you and Ryan can have the full run of the third floor. You can set things up differently or keep it the way we have it. Either way, Ryan will have more room to run around, and there's a door to keep him from heading down the stairs when you don't want him to get away from you."

Jessica laughed. "No doubt he'll figure doors out soon enough."

"I think we could safely conclude," Devon said, pointing to a rough drawing he'd made of the house, "that we could have six rooms to offer to guests. We could even offer the bunkhouse's extra beds if someone wanted to come out and truly experience the life of a ranch hand. Those articles Jessica brought from back East said that some folks actually pay money to be abused that way."

He grinned and poked Buck lightly in the ribs. "A drafty room, work from sunup to sundown, dirt and grit everywhere, and the smell of sweat and horses and cattle — yes sir, that's the kind of stuff I want to pay out good money to experience."

"You get to experience it for free," Jessica chided.

"But when we're back on our feet, I expect to be paid," Devon replied, looking at her in a way that made Jessica's pulse quicken. Oh, but he was handsome. She loved the way the summer sun had lightened his hair and tanned his face.

"I doubt that will happen for a while. Every dime we make is going to have to go back into making the ranch successful again."

"I wasn't necessarily talking about being paid in money," Devon said, his lips curling into a grin.

Buck snorted, and Kate turned away, but not before Jessica saw her smiling. They were all so conspiratorial in their teasing, and sometimes Jessica felt oddly left out. She had come onto the scene after they were all good friends, and sometimes it made her feel very uncomfortable. Like they all knew a good joke and refused to tell her.

"Well, it's getting late," Buck said, getting up from his chair. "I suspect Katie and I should retire for the evening. You two going to church in the morning?"

"Planning on it. I figured to drive Jessica and Ryan. You two need a lift?"

"No," Buck answered. "I figure on preaching a bit myself. Those ranch hands of ours need to get some religion now and then. What with the fact that it'll soon be time to herd those prime steers of ours to market, I

138

figure on giving them a couple of pointers on staying out of trouble."

Kate joined Buck, leaving Devon and Jessica alone in the front parlor. "See you both tomorrow. I figure on frying up a mess of chicken for the hands and for us as well. Anything else you're hungry for?"

Devon grinned. "How about some of your famous raspberry cream cake?"

Jessica threw Kate a quizzical look. "I don't think I've ever had that. Do you mean to tell me I've been here almost a year and never once had the opportunity to taste your 'famous raspberry cream cake'?"

Kate laughed. "It's only famous to Devon. But sure, I'll fix us up some. The raspberries came on real good this year. I'll bet those bushes down by the main springs are still bearing fruit."

"Maybe Jess and I could pick some for you after church tomorrow," Devon offered.

"Maybe you could just speak for yourself," Jessica added in mock ire.

"You two can work it out," Kate replied as Buck slipped his arm around her waist. "I'll see you tomorrow."

When they'd gone, Jessica turned back to find Devon still grinning at her. "What?"

"I don't know what you mean."

"You're looking at me oddly," Jessica

replied. She liked the way he was looking at her but refused to allow herself to show it. Devon's weekly trips into Cottonwood Falls had convinced her that he had a girlfriend in town. She tried not to think about it, but it bothered her nevertheless.

Devon chuckled and got up from his chair. "How about a stroll to the ridge? The moon is full, and the air warm."

"I can't," Jessica replied nervously. She was desperately afraid of being alone for too long with Devon. Just thinking about the ride into town for church caused her stomach to do flips.

"Why not?"

"Well, I should stay close to the house in case Ryan needs me."

"Guess that makes sense. So how about just coming out on the porch with me? The upstairs windows are open. You'll be able to hear him if he cries."

Jessica realized that she'd either have to be rude and refuse or go along with the plan. "All right. Maybe for a little bit. Then I need to go to bed."

He nodded and allowed her to lead the way to the front door. Neither one said another word until they were out on the porch. Devon and Buck had made some wonderful chairs and a couple benches, and it was to one of the latter that Devon motioned Jessica to follow him.

Nervously licking her lips, Jessica joined Devon on the bench. She put herself at the far edge of the seat, hoping Devon would take the hint and sit at the opposite end. He didn't, however, choosing instead to position himself right in the middle of the bench.

"It's a fine night," he said. Suddenly he jumped up. "Say, wait here. I have a surprise."

Jessica couldn't imagine what he had in mind, but she obediently nodded and watched as he bounded down the porch steps and disappeared around the side of the house. When he returned, he was carrying a guitar.

"I didn't know you played," she said in complete surprise.

"I just got started last winter. I've been taking lessons in town from Old Mr. Wiedermeier. That man can pick up anything and make music with it."

Jessica smiled as she wondered if it was this, and not a woman, that had been taking Devon to town on Friday evenings. It made her heart a little lighter, and she suddenly found herself quite eager to hear Devon play.

He began tuning the strings, strumming one and then another, then comparing the two to each other. When he finally had all six in agreeable harmony, he began strumming out a melody that Jessica instantly recognized.

"Why that sounds like 'O Worship the King.' "

Devon laughed. "That's good. It's supposed to." He played a few more bars.

"Do you sing as well?"

"I don't know about how *well* I do it, but I do sing." He didn't wait for her to ask but instead began to harmonize with the guitar. Devon's rich baritone rang out against the stillness of the night and stirred Jessica's heart. How lovely to sit on the porch in the warmth of late summer and listen to Devon sing. She could easily picture herself doing this for many years to come. Seeing it in her mind, she imagined herself married to Devon with four or five children gathered round them. It made a pleasant image to carry in her heart.

"I don't think I've ever seen such a look of contentment on your face, Miss Jessica," Devon drawled.

Jessica realized she'd just been caught daydreaming. "I was just thinking about something."

Devon put the guitar aside and moved closer to Jessica. "I've been doing some thinking, too. There's something I want to say to you."

Just then, the sound of Ryan crying reached Jessica's ears. "Oh, that's Ryan. I guess I'd better go."

Devon looked at her with such an expression of frustration and disappointment that Jessica very nearly sat back down. But her own nervousness held her fast. "I'll see you in the morning," she paused as if trying to decide whether or not she should say the rest, "and we can talk on the way to church."

With that she hurried upstairs, anxious and curious about what Devon might have had to tell her. Perhaps she was wrong about his trips into town. Maybe there was more than just the guitar lesson. Maybe her earlier feelings of Devon meeting up with a lady friend were more on target than she wanted to imagine.

By the time she'd reached Ryan, he'd fallen back to sleep and lay contentedly sucking his thumb. Jessica tidied his covers, gently touched his cheek with her fingers, and went back to her own room.

"There's something I want to say to you," Devon had said. The words were still ring-

ing in her ears.

What could he possibly need to say?

Devon knew nothing but frustration that Sunday morning. He'd barely slept a wink the night before, and now the horses were uncooperative as he tried to ready the buckboard wagon. He knew it wouldn't be nearly as comfortable for Jessica and Ryan, but there were supplies he'd been unable to bring home on Friday night, and he'd need this opportunity to get them safely home before he headed to Kansas City with the sale cattle.

He kept rethinking what he'd nearly said to Jessica the night before. It should have been simple. Jessica was a widow going on two years, and by her own declaration she'd never loved her husband. It seemed more than enough time to put the past behind her and deal with Devon's interests.

"Say, after church you might want to ask Joe Riley if he still wants to buy that acreage on the western boundaries of Windridge," Buck said as he came into the barn. He saw the difficulty Devon was having and immediately went to work to see the task completed.

"I'll do that," Devon said absentmindedly. "I'll ask Jessica if she's still of a mind to sell. You know how angry she gets when we try to question her."

"Still, she's a good-hearted woman," Buck replied.

"Yeah, I know that well enough," Devon muttered.

"You ain't gonna let that little gal get away from you, are you? There's plenty of fellows down at that church who'd give their right arms to be able to spend time with Jessie the way you do."

"For all the good it does."

"You feeling sorry for yourself, son?" Buck questioned. "That doesn't hardly seem like you."

"Not sure I even know what's like me anymore," Devon admitted. He took hold of the horses' harnesses and led the two matched geldings from the barn. "I wouldn't have been of a mind to turn this place into a dude ranch ten months ago, but look at me now."

"You just see the wisdom in it," Buck replied. "Besides, ranching and courting are two different things. I know you have feelings for Jessie. Why not just tell her and let the chips fall where they will?"

"I tried to say something last night, but —"

"Here we are," Jessica announced, coming

down the steps with Kate and Ryan directly behind her. Jessica stashed a small bag of necessities behind the wagon seat, then beamed Devon a smile that nearly broke his heart. How could a woman look so pretty and not even realize what she did to a fellow? She had a face like an angel. Long dark lashes, delicately arched brows. A straight little nose that turned up ever so slightly at the end, and lips so full and red that Devon was hard-pressed not to steal a kiss.

"We're all ready. Say, why are we taking the buckboard?" Jessica asked, letting Buck help her up onto the seat. She reached down and lifted Ryan from Kate's arms.

"Devon's picking up some supplies that came in on Friday. He didn't have the wagon with him when he went into town Friday night, so he secured them at the train station until he could pick them up today."

"No doubt someone will frown on his toting home necessities on the Lord's Day," Kate murmured. "But if we don't get some flour and sugar soon, not to mention coffee, we'll have a mutiny on our hands."

"No one will think anything about it," Devon said, climbing up to sit beside Jessica. The buckboard seat was very narrow and pushed the two people very close together. Devon could smell her perfume.

"If they have a problem with it, they can answer to me." With that he smacked the reins against the backs of the geldings.

The trip into town passed by before Devon and Jessica could get past discussing how they were going to renovate the house for their guests. Jessica had all manner of thoughts on the matter, and it seemed she and Kate had made some definite decisions. Each room would have a color theme with quilts and curtains to match. And guests would share breakfast together, which meant the extra extensions for the dining room table would have to be located and additional chairs ordered to match the existing ones.

Church hardly presented itself as a place to explain his feelings. Devon went through the motions of worship and even managed to focus his attention on the sermon, but over and over he thought of how he might share his feelings with Jessica. He was due to leave with the cattle in little more than two weeks, yet so much needed his attention, and very little time would be afforded him for quiet, romantic talks.

After church, Devon loaded up the ranch supplies while Jessica fed Ryan. Fussy and cantankerous from a day of being cooped up, Ryan seemed to do his level best to make life difficult for his mother. Jessica said he was teething, and she had it on Kate's authority that chewing a leather strap was the best thing to ease the pain. She'd brought one along just for this purpose and was trying to interest Ryan in chewing on it. Ryan just slapped at it and cried. Devon shook his head and finished securing two rolls of bailing wire before jumping up to take the reins.

"I imagine he'll be a whole lot happier when we get home," Devon suggested. He could see exasperation in Jessica's expression.

"I suppose you're right."

"You want me to hold him awhile?" he asked, seeing Ryan push and squirm while crying at the top of his lungs.

To his surprise, Jessica shrugged, then handed the boy over. Ryan instantly calmed and took notice of Devon's mustache. "Now, partner, we're going to have to have an understanding here. I'm driving this here wagon, and you're going to have to help me." He showed Ryan the leather reins, and immediately the boy put them in his mouth.

"No!" Jessica began, then shook her head and relaxed. "Oh, might as well let him. I found him eating dirt yesterday. Guess a little sweat and leather won't hurt."

Devon laughed. "It could be a whole lot worse." He called to the horses and started them for home while Ryan played with the extra bit of reins.

Jessica watched them both for several moments, and Devon could sense she felt troubled by the situation. They rode in silence for several miles while Devon battled within himself. The selfish side of him wanted to just get his feelings out in the open — to express how he felt about Jessica and the boy he held on his lap. But the more humanitarian side of him figured it was only right to find out what was troubling Jessica.

"You're mighty quiet. You going to tell me what it's all about?" Devon finally worked up the nerve to ask.

Jessica looked at him blankly for a moment. Then he noticed there were tears in her eyes. She shook her head, sniffled, and looked away.

Ryan's head began to nod, and Devon figured it the perfect excuse to draw her focus back to him. "I think someone's about to fall asleep. You want to take him back?"

Jessica smoothed the lines of her emerald-green suit and reached out for her son. Ryan went to her without protest, and Devon thought Jessica looked almost relieved. She cradled the boy in her arms, and Ryan willingly let her rock him back and forth. Within another mile or two, he'd fallen asleep without so much as a whimper.

Devon tried to figure out what Jessica's display of emotions had been about. He'd never been around women for very long. Even his mother and sister, who now lived a world away in Tyler, Texas, always kept to themselves when emotional outbursts were at hand. His mother had always said such things were not to be shared with their menfolk, but Devon disagreed. He worried about those times when his mother went off to cry alone. His father always seemed to be away working one ranch or another, always someone else's hired man. He seldom knew about his wife's tears or needs, and Devon determined it would be different with him — mostly because he knew how painful it was for his mother to bear such matters alone.

He could remember the time when his younger brother, Danny, had still been alive. Pa had gone off to work on the Double J Ranch, hoping to earn extra money before the winter set in. Danny had contracted whooping cough and died within a week of their father's departure. His mother had borne the matter with utmost grace and confidence. Devon tried to be the man of the house for her, supporting her at the funeral, seeing to her needs afterwards. But she would have no part of sharing her pain with him, and it hurt Devon deeply to be left out. When their father had returned, his mother had simply said, "We are only four now." Nothing more was mentioned or discussed. At least not in front of Devon.

Unable to take the situation without pushing to understand, Devon looked over at Jessica. He watched her for a moment before saying, "Please tell me what's bothering you."

Jessica continued to stare straight ahead. Her expression suggested that she was strongly considering his request. Finally she answered. "It isn't worth troubling you with."

"How about letting me be the judge of that?"

They continued for nearly another ten minutes before Jessica finally answered. "I can't hope that you would understand. It has to do with being a mother."

"I suppose I can't understand what it is to be a mother," Devon agreed, "but I do understand when someone is hurting, and you are obviously in pain."

Jessica nestled Ryan closer to her in a protective manner, and instantly Devon realized that her mood had to do with her insecurities over the boy. He'd figured she'd outgrown her concerns, but apparently she still carried the weight of her fears with her.

"Are you still afraid of losing his affection?" Devon finally asked.

Jessica stiffened for a moment, then her shoulders slumped forward as if she'd just met her defeat. "You can't understand."

"I only held him to help calm him down. You looked so tired, and Ryan was obviously tired; I just figured it might help."

"It did help," she said, wiping at tears with her free hand. "It's just that he's all I have, Devon. If I can't be a good mother to him — if I can't make it work between us — then I might as well give up."

"Give up what? Motherhood? You can't take them back once they're here."

"But there are those who would take them from you," Jessica declared.

Devon felt confused. Who did she fear would take Ryan from her? "You don't mean to suggest that someone might come after Ryan, do you? Someone from back East? His grandparents? Is that it?"

Jessica shook her head. "Newman's family is all dead. They died when he was a teen-ager. His only brother died some years after that. He'd never married, and therefore

Newman was the end of the line."

"Then who?"

Jessica still refused to look Devon in the face. "There was a friend in New York, Essie. She always offered to help me with Ryan. She always insisted on having us spend our days with her, and she never wanted me to lift a finger to care for Ryan. She made me uneasy, but I felt sorry for her. She was barren, you see."

Devon did indeed begin to get a clear picture of what must have taken place. "Go on," he urged.

Jessica ran her hand across Ryan's head. "One day she came to me with the idea of letting her and her husband adopt Ryan. She said it was impossible for me to give Ryan all he needed. She said she would make a better mother."

"She obviously didn't know you very well," Devon muttered.

Jessica turned and gave him a look of frantic gratitude. "She thought she did. I'm afraid I was rather harsh with her and sent her home with her suggestion completely refused. Two days later, her mother showed up on my doorstep. The woman was positively intimidating. She took one look at my home and condemned it. She said it would be a wonder if Ryan weren't dead by winter."

Devon clamped his teeth together in anger. He wanted to say something to counter the horrible insensitivity of the woman's actions, but he knew there was nothing he could do.

"She finally left, but then Essie showed up the next day and the next day and the day after that. Ryan adored her because she spoiled and pampered him. I began to fear that he loved her more than me, and when I sent her from my home for the last time, I had to forcibly remove Ryan from her arms. He cried and cried, and Essie cried and declared it a sign that she should be his true mother. I told her to never come back, and I slammed the door on her. Three days later, the letter came announcing Father's death. It seemed like an answer from God, and yet I would have never wished my father dead. I'd just about decided to beg him to let me return to Windridge anyway."

"But Jess, she can't hurt you," Devon said, hoping his words would comfort her. "She's far enough away that she can't just drop in on you and make you miserable again. And Kate would never tolerate anyone storming into Windridge and threatening yours and Ryan's happiness. This Essie can't hurt you anymore."

Jessica said nothing for several moments. Then she shifted Ryan in her arms and looked at Devon with an expression of intense pain. "But you can."

Devon felt the wind go out from him. "What?" he barely managed to ask.

"Ryan adores you. He seeks you out, and he's drawn to you like flies to honey. I can't ignore that. I can't just look away and say it doesn't exist. Neither can I find it in myself to deny him."

"Why would you want to? You have nothing to fear from me. I'm completely devoted to the little guy. I wouldn't do anything to hurt him or you."

"Maybe not willingly," Jessica replied. She looked away, and Devon watched as she fixed her sight on the horizon where the house on Windridge was now coming into view.

Devon wanted to reassure her and thought for a moment about declaring his feelings for her, but it didn't seem right. Somehow he feared she would just presume he'd made it all up to comfort her. Feeling at a loss as to what he could say, Devon said nothing at all. He looked heavenward for a moment, whispered a prayer for guidance, then fixed his sight on the road ahead. Somehow, someway, God would show him what he was to do about Jessica and Ryan.

CHAPTER 7

Driving cattle had always been a loathsome chore to Devon. He didn't like the time spent with cantankerous animals on the dusty trail, and he certainly didn't care for being away from Windridge. Especially now. Leaving Jessica wouldn't be easy, and Devon tried to avoid thinking of how he would handle their good-bye.

The days passed too quickly to suit him, and before he knew it, Devon was giving instructions to the other four ranch hands, explaining how they would drive the cattle to Cottonwood Falls and from there board the train for Kansas City.

"I'll only need you as far as Cottonwood. You all get two weeks to settle any other business you have." He pointed to two of the cowhands. "Sam and Joe can take off after we get the livestock settled in the freight cars. Neil, you and Bob need to wait until the other two get back. Buck will handle the ranch until I return, which hopefully won't be any longer than two, maybe three weeks."

The men nodded, asked their questions, and waited for Devon to dismiss them to prepare for the drive. "We'll head out in fifteen minutes or so. Be ready."

The men moved off to collect their horses just as Buck ambled up. "Heard tell the Johnsons down Wichita way are working with a new breed," Buck said as Devon finished packing his bags. "You could go down that way before coming back here. You know, check it out and see if it would work for us."

"I suppose I could. But do you think that's the direction we want to go?" Devon questioned, not liking the idea of delaying his return to Windridge.

Buck shrugged. "It's just an idea. Heard they're getting an extra twenty to fifty pounds on the hoof. You can suit yourself though."

"I'll give it some consideration. Maybe I'll find the same thing in Kansas City. Most folks in these parts are going to end up at the livestock yards there anyway. It just might work out I can get the information there."

Buck nodded. "That sounds reasonable."

Kate appeared just then, Ryan toddling behind her. "I brought you some sandwiches to take with you. I know you don't have that long of a drive, but those animals can be mighty slow when they set their minds to be that way."

"Thanks, Katie," Devon said, taking the basket she'd packed. "If we don't need them, I'll take some of them to Kansas City."

"Eat my sandwiches instead of Mr. Harvey's fine railroad food?" Kate laughed. "I can't imagine anyone making that trade."

"Then you just don't realize what a good cook you are," Devon replied. About that time, Ryan wrapped his arms around Devon's leg and started chattering.

"Horsy! Horsy!"

Devon laughed. He often gave the boy a ride on his knee, and it was clear Ryan wasn't about to let him leave until he received his daily fun.

"Okay," he said, reaching down to lift Ryan into the air. He swept the boy high, listening to his giggles, then circled him down low. Finally he stepped over to a bale of hay and sat down to put Ryan on his knee. "Now tighten those legs," Devon instructed, squeezing Ryan's legs around his own. "A good rider knows how to use

159

his legs."

"You keep an eye on him for a minute," Buck called out. "I'm going to walk a spell with Katie and tell her good-bye properly."

"Will do," Devon called out, "but you won't be gone for more than a few hours."

Buck laughed. "To Kate, that's an eternity."

Devon, too, chuckled and returned his attention to Ryan. "You know, you'll be a right fine rider one day. I'll take you out on the trails and teach you all there is to know about raising cattle. You'll know more than your ma or anyone else in these parts, 'cause I'm going to show you all the tricks."

Ryan giggled and squealed with delight as Devon bounced him up and down on his leg. The boy had easily taken a huge chunk of Devon's heart, while the other portion belonged to his mother. The only real problem was finding a way to tell her.

Devon had fully planned to discuss his feelings for Jessica before he left for Kansas City. But the opportunity never presented itself. Jessica had been overly busy under Kate's instruction, and when she wasn't working at quilting or sewing or any number of other things Kate deemed necessary to her ranch training, Jessica was busy with Ryan. She almost always retired early, not even giving Devon a chance to suggest a stroll on the ridge or a song or two on the porch. The only time she went into town was on Sunday, and that was usually with Buck and Kate at her side. Devon had no desire to make his confession of feelings a public issue. Even if Buck and Kate already presumed to know those feelings, Devon wanted to get Jessica's reaction first.

"Well Ryan, a fellow just never knows where he stands," Devon muttered.

Ryan seemed to understand and chattered off several strange words, along with his repertoire of completely understandable speech. "More horsy! Mama horsy."

Devon laughed. "I doubt Mama would appreciate the idea, son." The word *son* stuck in his throat. He wished he could call Ryan son. He thought of Jessica's worries that he would steal Ryan's affections, but in truth, Devon worried that Jessica would take Ryan from his life. He already cared too much about both of them, and the thought of losing either one was more than he wanted to contend with.

Lifting Ryan in his arms, Devon rubbed his fuzzy head. "You've got to grow some more hair, boy. You don't want to go through life bald." Ryan reached out and pulled at Devon's thick mustache. "Ah, a mustache man. Well, grow it there if you prefer," Devon teased, "but the head would be better for now."

He gently disentangled his mustache from Ryan's pudgy fingers, then gave the boy a couple of gentle tosses into the air. Ryan squealed once again, and the expression on his chubby face was enough to satisfy Devon.

"You take good care of your mama while I'm gone," Devon told him and hugged him close.

"Kate said you two were in here," called Jessica.

Devon looked up, almost embarrassed to have been caught speaking of her. He wondered how long she'd been watching. She looked to have been there for some time, given her casual stance by the open door.

"We were just having a talk," Devon said, putting Ryan down.

"Horsy, Mama," Ryan said, toddling off to Jessica's waiting arms.

She lifted Ryan and held him close and all the while watched Devon. "Are you about ready to go?"

"Yup," he said casually, taking down an extra coil of rope from the wall. "Everything's set. We have to give ourselves enough time to make the train."

Jessica nodded. "Well, I hope you won't have any trouble finding everything we need."

"I shouldn't," Devon replied, wishing they could get beyond the chitchat.

Ryan began squirming and calling for Devon. The boy had not yet mastered Devon's name, so when he called out, it sounded very much like "Da da."

"Unt Da da," Ryan fussed, straining at Jessica's hold. She put the boy down, not even attempting to fight Ryan's choice.

The boy hurried back to Devon, inspected the rope for a moment, then raised his arms up and bobbed up and down as if to encourage Devon to lift him.

"It's easy to see how much he loves you," Jessica said, her voice low and filled with emotion.

"I love him, too," Devon said, wondering how she would react to this. "He's a great little guy. It would be impossible *not* to love him."

Jessica nodded. "I just hope you take that love seriously."

"What do you mean?" Devon asked, wishing he could turn the conversation to thoughts of his feelings for Ryan's mother.

Jessica stepped closer and studied Devon

before answering. "I just ask one thing of you, Devon Carter. Don't let Ryan get close to you unless you plan to be around to be his friend for a good long time. It'll be too hard for him otherwise."

At first, Devon wanted to reply with something flippant and teasing, but he could see in Jessica's eyes that she was dead serious. His heart softened, and he gave her a weak smile.

"I plan to be around for a very long time. I wouldn't dream of leaving Ryan without making sure he understood my reason for leaving. And since he'll be too small to understand much along those lines and will be for a good many years, I guess you'll both just be stuck with me."

"Just so you understand."

He rubbed the boy's head, kissed him lightly, and put him back on the ground. "I intend to always be here for Ryan," Devon stated firmly. He looked deep into Jessica's dark eyes — knowing the longing reflected there. He wanted more than anything to add that he would also be there for Jessica, but he could already hear Buck calling everyone to mount up.

"Guess you'd better go," Jessica whispered.

Devon took a step toward her, then

stopped. There wasn't enough time to say what he wanted — needed — to say. "I suppose so," he finally murmured.

"You've got the list?" she questioned.

He nodded, almost afraid to say anything more.

"And you will be careful?"

Her voice was edged with concern, and Devon longed to put her worried mind at ease. He remembered that moment months ago when he'd held her while she cried. "It's a piece of cake," he replied. "The hard part is getting the critters to Cottonwood. After that, there's nothing to it but haggling the money." He grinned, hoping to put her at ease.

"I've heard about folks killed in stampedes," she countered. "And Kate says we're coming up to time for a tornado or two."

"We'll be careful," he promised, realizing that whether she spoke it in words or not, she cared about his well-being.

"You coming?" Buck asked as he poked his head into the doorway.

Devon caught his mischievous expression and sighed. "I'm coming."

Jessica had the distinct impression that had Buck not interfered, Devon might have said something very important. She sensed his desire to tell her something, but no matter how long she stood there in silence, he seemed unable to spit out the words. Of course she did no better. She had hoped to say that her concerns for Ryan were based on concerns she also felt for herself. She knew she was coming to depend too much on Devon. She also knew that she'd lost her heart to him, and that for the first and only time in her life, she was in love.

With this thought still weighing heavily on her heart, Jessica followed Devon from the barn, calling to Ryan as she moved back to the house. She picked the boy up and told him to wave good-bye to Devon.

"Unta go," Ryan began to whine. "Me go, too."

"No, Ryan," Jessica said. "You have to stay here. We can't go this time."

Ryan continued to fuss, and Katie tried to still him with a cookie that she kept in her apron pocket for just such occasions. Ryan contented himself with the treat, while Jessica found no such consolation.

I should have told him how I felt, she thought. But her feelings were so foreign and new to her that she wasn't sure what she would have said to him.

"I should be back by the end of November," Devon called to them, bringing his horse to a halt just beyond the porch. "Don't worry though if I'm later than that. It may take some time to secure the freighters and collect all the things you ladies have deemed necessary to running a good resort."

"Do you have the money?" Jessica asked.

"I'll pick up most of it in Cottonwood Falls. I have the deed papers for Joe Riley's piece of land, and that will allow me to take his money for the land and add to what we have in the bank." He glanced over his shoulder and saw that Buck was already positioning the ranch hands in preparation for moving the cattle from the corrals. "I'd best get over there and do my job." He turned the horse and started to leave.

"Devon!" Jessica called out. She knew her voice sounded desperate, but she couldn't help it.

He stopped, looked at her quite seriously, then grinned. "What?"

Jessica swallowed hard and tried to think of something neutral to say. "I'll be praying for you," she finally managed.

Devon's grin broadened. "Thanks. With that bunch," he said, motioning over his shoulder, "I'll need it." He took off before either Kate or Jessica could say another word.

"Wonder whether he means the men or the steers?" Kate teased.

"Probably both."

Jessica brushed cookie crumbs from Ryan's face and headed to the front door when Kate called out, "Looks like we have company."

Turning, Jessica could see the faint image of a black carriage making its way up the Windridge road. "Who could that be?"

Kate shrugged. "I don't know. I'll go put some tea on and set out some more cookies. It's been so long since anyone's come calling at Windridge, I might not even be able to find a serving plate."

Jessica laughed. "Don't you go running off when whoever it is finally arrives. I don't want to have to entertain on my own."

"Maybe we could set up things in the quilting room," Kate suggested and Jessica nodded.

"Sounds perfect. That way, we'll be busy, and if the conversation lags, we can talk about the quilts."

Kate nodded. "Why don't you put Ryan down for a nap in the back room? Then he'll be close at hand and yet out of harm's way."

Jessica nodded and followed Kate into the

house, after sending one final glance south where Devon and the rest of the ranch hands were organizing the cattle on the trail. Giving Ryan a drink of milk while Kate fixed the tea, Jessica made her way into one of the two rooms that were being converted for Buck and Kate's use. It had been Kate's idea to put another bed in for Ryan. It seemed senseless to run up and down the stairs all day, and Jessica quickly saw the sense in it. Kate had even suggested that maybe Jessica and Ryan would one day prefer the privacy of the cottage once the guests overtook the house. Jessica had quickly pointed out that Devon now occupied the place in question, but Kate had just shrugged and told her that God had a way of working those things out.

"But the way I'd like to see it worked out," Jessica told Ryan, "isn't likely to happen. Devon said God already has a wife picked out for him."

Ryan yawned and pulled at his ear. This was his routine signal that he was tired. Gently, she tucked him into bed and brushed his cheek with her fingertip. Ryan quickly realized she intended to leave him for a nap and decided he wanted no part of it. Jessica wasn't surprised at the display as he began kicking at the covers. Soon he was sitting up and fussing for her to take him.

"Ryan," she said in a stern voice. "You lie back down and go to sleep. When you get up, we'll go up to the ridge and see what we can see."

Ryan made no move to obey, so Jessica gently eased him back down and pulled the covers around him once again. "Now go to sleep and be a good boy."

"Goo boy," Ryan muttered in between his fussing.

"That's right," Jessica smiled. "You are a good boy, and Mama loves you."

She left him there to fuss and upon returning to the kitchen found that Kate had things well under control. "Is there anything you want me to do?" she questioned.

"No. Just relax."

Jessica looked out the side kitchen window, hoping to catch a glimpse of the cattle drive. She could just catch sight of the last two outriders, but Devon was nowhere in sight. She strained her eyes for some sign of his brown Stetson, but the hills hid him from view.

"You should have told him how you feel about him," Kate admonished. Jessica felt her face grow hot as she looked back to where Kate studied her. "It's pretty apparent."

"I didn't realize," Jessica admitted. "You don't suppose he knows, do you?" She realized her voice sounded high pitched, almost frightened.

"No, I don't suppose he does," Kate replied, turning back to putting cookies on the tray. "I think he's too wrapped up in his own feelings."

Jessica nodded. "I think you're probably right."

"Why don't you go check on our visitor? Ought to be up to the house by now."

Jessica did as Kate suggested, her heart heavy with thoughts of Devon being in love with another woman. When she opened the front door, she was surprised to find a smartly dressed woman making her way up the front steps of the porch.

The woman, looking to be in her late forties, carried herself with a regal air. Her golden-blond hair, although liberally sprinkled with gray, was carefully styled and pinned tightly beneath a beautiful bonnet of lavender silk.

"Good morning," Jessica said, trying her best to sound welcoming.

"Good morning to you," the woman replied. "I'm Gertrude Jenkins, and you must be Jessica Gussop."

"Albright. Jessica Albright. Gussop was

my maiden name."

"Of course. I remember Gus having quite a spell when you married."

Jessica felt her defenses rise to the occasion. "We don't get many visitors here, Mrs. Jenkins. Won't you come in?"

The woman smiled. "I used to come here quite often, you know, before Gus died. After he died, I went on an extended European trip. Couldn't bear to stick around here with him gone, don't you know?"

Jessica couldn't figure the woman out. She'd never heard of Gertrude Jenkins, much less in any capacity that endeared her to her father. She ushered the woman into the house and, rather than stopping at the front parlor, led her down the hall to the room she and Kate used for quilting. Kate already sat sewing behind the quilting frame, while Jessica's work lay on the seat of the chair nearest to Kate. It looked for all intents and purposes that Jessica had only moments before left the work in order to answer the door.

"Well, if it isn't Gerty Jenkins," Kate said in greeting. "I heard tell you were back in the area." Jessica watched the exchange between the two women, feeling the immediate tension when Gertrude spotted Kate.

"Hello, Kate," came the crisp reply. She glanced around the room and sniffed. "Well, if this isn't quaint."

"We've been working on quilts. We were just going to have some tea and cookies," Jessica offered rather formally. "I do hope you can stay and partake with us?"

Gertrude glanced to the small table where the refreshments awaited their attention. "I'm certain I can. Especially after coming all this way."

"Gerty lives on the ranch directly south," Kate told Jessica. "It's her drive you pass by on the way to church."

Jessica smiled and nodded. "I remember Devon mentioning the drive leading to another ranch."

"Devon? Devon Carter?" Gertrude questioned. "Don't tell me he's still here at Windridge."

"Of course he is," Kate replied before Jessica could answer. "He was like a son to Gus, and Jessica has come to rely on him as well."

Gertrude eyed Jessica rather haughtily as she pulled white kid gloves from her hands. "I suppose it is difficult when you know nothing of ranching."

Jessica could immediately see that Gertrude had no intention of being a friend.

But her reasons for visiting in the first place were still a mystery.

Ignoring the comment, Jessica motioned to a high-backed chair. "Won't you sit down? I'll pour the tea."

"Cream and sugar, please," Gertrude stated as she took her seat.

Jessica nodded and went to the task. "Would you care for some of Kate's sugar cookies? They're quite delicious."

"If you have no cakes, I suppose they'll have to do," the woman replied.

Jessica served her and then brought a cup of plain tea to Kate. She tried to question Kate with her expression, but Kate only smiled.

"I suppose I should have visited sooner," Gertrude continued before anyone else could take up the conversation, "but I've only returned last week. A year abroad has done me a world of good."

"This last year has done us a world of good as well," Kate replied, continuing with her stitches.

Jessica thought the response rather trite given Kate's usual friendliness, but she said nothing. Instead, she tried to draw out the reason for Gertrude's visit. "I'm pleased you have found the time to call upon us," Jessica began. "I don't believe we've had a single visitor in the past year."

"Well, it really is no wonder. The place is in an awful state of disrepair."

"Oh," Jessica said, looking first to Kate, then back to Gertrude, "you must not have had the opportunity to look around you. We've been making steady progress throughout the year. We are, in fact, moving ahead with plans to turn Windridge into something rather special."

"Well, it once was quite special," Gertrude said, flicking crumbs from her skirt onto the floor. "Do tell, what plans have you for the place?"

Jessica licked her lips and took the tiniest sip of tea to steady her nerves. "We're opening Windridge to the public. We are taking on guests next summer and becoming a working vacation ranch. A quiet respite from the city, if you will."

Gertrude appeared stunned. "Are you suggesting this place will become a spa — a resort? Here in Kansas?"

"Not only suggesting it, Gerty," Kate threw in, "but the plans are already in the works. Devon is bringing back the final touches in new furnishings and supplies."

"Was that him heading out with that scrawny herd?"

"Him and Buck and the others," Kate

replied. "Only Devon is heading on to Kansas City. He figured we'd best keep the others here to keep an eye on things."

"Yes, but who will keep an eye on Devon Carter?"

Jessica perked up at this. "Whatever do you mean?"

"I simply mean, my dear," Gertrude began, "the man should not be trusted."

"Bah," Kate said in disgust. "Gus trusted him."

"Yes, and see where it got him."

"I don't think I understand," Jessica interjected, feeling the anger between the two women.

"Gerty is just showing her age." All eyes turned to Kate at this. "Gerty's daughter was once engaged to Devon, but she broke it off."

"She had to. There was simply no other choice under the circumstances," Gertrude said stiffly.

Jessica felt the tension mount. She silently wished Kate would stir the woman into another subject of conversation, but Gertrude remained fixed on her mark.

"Devon was seen with another woman in Cottonwood Falls. Of course, my poor Jane was devastated. They were barely two weeks away from their own wedding. It grieved her so much she stayed out the entire night and came home weeping in the wee hours of the morning."

Kate rolled her eyes, and Jessica was hard-pressed not to smile. Apparently Kate thought the story to be less than accurate, but Gertrude didn't seem to notice. "I was heartsick, and had her father still been alive, he would no doubt have gone to take Devon Carter to task for his behavior.

"Poor Jane cried until she was exhausted, then told me she had found Devon in the arms of another woman." Gertrude leaned closer. "He was kissing her, don't you know? Of course, Jane felt terribly misused. She was never herself after that and ran off with the first man who asked for her hand after Devon's terrible behavior."

"That wasn't exactly the story we heard," Kate muttered under her breath.

Gertrude glared at her but said nothing to support the idea that her version was anything but the honest facts of the matter.

"I simply wouldn't trust him out of sight, my dear. Gus and I discussed it on many an occasion, and while Gus felt the need to give the young man a chance, I always felt there was something rather shiftless about him."

"You let Jane get engaged to him," Kate

threw out.

"Yes," Gertrude replied in a clipped tone, "but then every mother makes mistakes. I wanted Jane's happiness, and she was certain Devon Carter could give her everything she desired."

Jessica felt shaken and uncertain of herself. She wondered if the other woman Jane had found Devon with was the same one who now held his heart. "More tea?" she asked weakly.

"No, thank you," Gertrude replied, setting the cup and saucer aside. "I really should be going. I can see that you both have your hands full, and there's much that needs my attention at home. I do recall someone mentioning, however, that you have a child, Mrs. Albright."

"That's right. My Ryan is almost two. He's sleeping right now, or I'd give you a proper introduction. Perhaps Sunday at church?"

"Yes, perhaps so," Gertrude replied, getting to her feet. "I do suggest you heed my advice. Devon Carter is not all he appears to be, and if you have given him a large sum of money, it might well be the last time you see him or your funds." She glanced at Kate. "Good day, Kate. Mrs. Albright."

Jessica walked out with the haughty

woman and paused on the porch. "Thank you for coming, Mrs. Jenkins."

"I felt I owed it to Gus. You know we were very close to an understanding. Had he lived, I'm certain I would be mistress of Windridge, and our ranches would join together to make a mighty empire."

Jessica did her best to show no signs of surprise at this announcement. She merely nodded and bid the woman good day.

Gertrude Jenkins climbed into her carriage and pulled on her gloves. "I suppose we will be seeing each other again soon. Don't forget what I said about Mr. Carter. It's not too late to send someone after him and change the course of events to come."

With that, she turned the horses and headed the buggy down the lane. Jessica watched for several moments, uncertain what to think or feel about the woman and her visit. Not only had Mrs. Jenkins discredited Devon, but she'd implied an intimacy with Jessica's father. An intimacy that suggested marriage. Jessica found it impossible to believe and thought to question Kate about it, but it was clear the two women had nothing but disdain for each other.

With a sigh, Jessica decided it wasn't worth the bother. She trusted Devon to do what he said he would do. Closing the door behind her, Jessica decided to close out negative thoughts of her visitor. She had no reason to worry and refused to borrow the trouble that Gertrude Jenkins so expertly offered.

CHAPTER 8

The first week without Devon at Windridge left Jessica feeling listless and bored. Kate kept her occupied with canning and butchering, but at night Jessica had nothing to keep her from thinking about Devon. Not only that, but Ryan cried and called for him, leaving Jessica little doubt that her fears about Ryan's attachment to the cowboy were well founded.

Week two spent itself out with the return of Sam and Joe and the departure of Neil and Bob. Jessica worked with Kate to make lye soap. Kate told her there was no sense in paying out good money for store-bought soap when they had the hog fat and other ingredients on hand. Jessica hated the work but realized she was doing something important to keep Windridge up and running. Soap was a necessity of life — especially if you intended to keep guests.

By the third week, Jessica began to watch

from her upstairs window for some sign of Devon's return. She mourned the loss along with her son and grew despondent and moody. Kate and Buck watched her with knowing smiles and tried their best to interest her in other things, but it was no use.

An early snow followed by a fierce ice storm caused Jessica to sink even lower. Now it was impossible to spend much time outside, and even horseback riding was curtailed. Making the hour journey into Cottonwood Falls was clearly out of the question, and so their boredom intensified.

Gertrude Jenkins's words kept intruding into Jessica's thoughts. She realized the older woman had planted seeds of doubt, and although Jessica was determined not to let them grow, Devon's delay seemed to bring about their germination. She wondered at Devon's past and why her father thought so highly of him. She wondered if Gertrude had known something about Devon that no one else had knowledge of. Maybe Jane Jenkins had truly seen Devon betraying her.

Jessica hated even allowing such thoughts, but as November passed and December came upon them and still there was no word from Devon Carter, she began to fear the worst.

"Buck says it looks to be nice for a few days," Kate told Jessica one morning. "He doesn't see any reason why we can't go in and participate in the ladies' Christmas quilt party."

"I don't feel like going," Jessica told Kate.

"I know. Which is exactly why we're going."

Jessica looked up from where she was busy washing the breakfast dishes. Kate had that determined look that told Jessica clearly she'd brook no nonsense in the matter.

"What about Ryan?" she asked, casting a glance at her son. At almost two years of age, Ryan was into everything, and it was too cold for him to travel the long distance into Cottonwood Falls.

"Buck is going to take care of him," Kate told her firmly.

"Buck?"

"Absolutely. He handled our own boys well enough. There's no reason at Ryan's age that Buck can't see to his needs. I've already talked with him, and Buck thinks it's a good idea. He knows how worried you are and how hard the waiting has been. Besides, Devon might even come in on the train while we're in town."

It was this last thought that made up Jessica's mind. "All right, let's do it."

Kate grinned. "I thought you'd see things my way."

But three hours later, Jessica wasn't at all sure that they should have come. The location for the sewing party rotated each year through the various families in the church and this time was at Esther Hammel's house. The living room had been cleared of furniture with the exception of wooden-backed chairs, a couple worktables, and several quilting frames.

This was an annual event for the women of Cottonwood Falls, and everyone took their duties quite seriously. One person came to help Esther set up the frames and worktables, while another was in charge of organizing the refreshments. Someone else held the responsibility of making sure the word got out as to the place and time, and yet another lady arranged a group of women to help with the cleanup.

Everyone brought food to the party, and Jessica was rather relieved to find that this was the only requirement she had to meet. Esther said that being as it was her first year to join them, they would go rather easy on her.

The women gathered, taking their places around the various work areas. Jessica and

Kate were in the process of piecing some quilt tops together, so they took seats at one of the worktables rather than at the frames. Esther Hammel, a petite woman with fiery blue eyes and a knotted bun of white hair, saw to it that everyone had all they needed in order to work before calling the women to order.

"First, we'll pray. Then we'll gab." Everyone smiled and nodded, while Esther bowed her head. "Father, we thank You for this beautiful day and for the fellowship of friends. Bless our work to better the lives of those around us. May we always bring You glory and honor. Amen."

Jessica murmured an amen, but her heart and mind were far from the prayer. She had hoped to see Devon by now. She had imagined how they would meet on the road to Cottonwood, and he would surprise her with a caravan of goods and supplies that would leave no one doubting his honesty and goodness. But they had met no one on the road between Windridge and Cottonwood.

Buck had instructed Sam to drive the massive stagelike carriage for the women. That way, they could enjoy the warmth and comfort of the plush furnishings. Sam had family in town and was only too happy to go home to his mother's cooking while waiting for Kate and Jessica. It was also rumored that his parents' neighbors had a fetching daughter who seemed to have an eye for Sam.

Jessica had instructed Sam to check on Devon at the railroad station, just in case there was some word from him. She'd also told him to pick up the Windridge mail and to check with the telegraph office, just in case some word had come in that they'd not yet received because of the weather. She could hardly sit still through the sewing for want of knowing whether Sam had found out anything about Devon.

"So when I finish with this quilt," Esther was telling the women gathered around her frame, "I intend to donate it to poor Sarah Newcome. Her Elmer died two weeks ago, and they're dirt poor. She's got another baby coming in the spring, and those other three kids of hers don't have proper clothes or bedding. I figured this here quilt could keep all three of them warm."

"My Christmas project was to make and finish five baby blankets for the new mothers in the area," spoke another woman. "As soon as I get this last one quilted, I'll probably start on my spring projects."

The chatter continued until it came to Jessica and Kate's turn to speak. Kate seemed to understand Jessica's confusion and took charge. "Jessica and I have had many projects this year. The latest one, however, is to put together a number of quilts to give to the orphans' home in Topeka."

Jessica said nothing, realizing that Kate had indeed mentioned the project some weeks ago, but since that had occurred around the time of Devon's departure, she'd totally forgotten what they were working toward.

"The quilt tops we're working on today are for the girls." Kate held up her piece to reveal carefully ordered flower baskets. The colors were done up in lavender and pink calicos, with pieces of green and baskets of gold. "I think we'll have them put together by Christmas, but whether or not we'll be able to get them shipped north will depend on the weather."

At this the women made comments on the weather and how the early snow hampered one thing or another. The ice had been the worst, they all agreed, and for several minutes that topic held the conversation. Jessica sighed and worked to put together her pieces in an orderly fashion. There were only a few weeks left before Christmas. Devon should have been home already, and yet here she sat, with no word from him and no idea as to his welfare.

A knock on the front door sent Esther off to find out who had arrived and caused Jessica to hold her breath in anticipation that the visitor might be Devon. Disappointment engulfed her, however, as the visitor proved to be Gertrude Jenkins.

"Sorry for being so late," Gertrude announced. "I had so much to take care of this morning that I just couldn't seem to get it all accomplished." Her gaze fell upon Jessica and Kate, and her pasted smile faded. "Well, if I'd have known you were planning on coming to the party, we could have shared transportation." Her voice sounded accusatory, as though Kate and Jessica had committed some sort of heinous crime.

"Sorry about that, Gerty," Kate replied without missing a beat. "We figured you'd still be all worn out from your travels abroad."

Jessica nearly smiled at this. She knew how artfully Kate had maneuvered Gertrude into her favorite topic. There'd be little more retribution for their lack of notification once Gertrude focused on her journeys.

"Oh, I suppose I'm still young enough to bounce right back from such things. I do admit at first I was quite exhausted, but a few days of rest and I felt quite myself again." She allowed Esther to take the pie pan she still held and then swept out of her coat and gloves and handed them to Esther just as she returned from the refreshment table.

"We were just commenting on the weather and our projects," Esther told her after seeing to Gertrude's coat and gloves.

Gertrude removed her ornate wool bonnet and set it aside on the fireplace mantel. "We suffered terribly from the ice," she admitted. "But as for my project, well, I simply haven't started one. I thought I'd come here and help someone else with theirs."

"Good," said Esther. "You can help us quilt. I've already told the girls, but my Christmas project is for Sarah Newcome."

Gertrude's chin lifted ever so slightly, but she said nothing as she took her seat at the quilting frame. After several moments of silence, someone finally asked her about her time in Paris, and the conversation picked back up with a detailed soliloquy.

"Of course," Gertrude said, eyeing Jessica suspiciously, "I was quite happy to arrive in Kansas City and make my connection for home." Without pausing for breath she added, "Speaking of Kansas City, has Devon returned with your supplies?"

Jessica felt the wind go out of her. She didn't know what to say that wouldn't provoke a new topic of conversation centered around the possibility that Devon had deserted ranks. Apparently this dilemma showed on her face, because Gertrude nodded and continued.

"I thought not. I hadn't heard from any of my hands that he'd made it back into town. Well, I certainly hope for your sake that he's at least notified you as to what's keeping him."

"No, Gerty, Devon doesn't need to check in with us," Kate responded. "He's family, and we trust him to be making the right choices. He left here with a long list of things to accomplish, and we don't expect him to return until he's able to negotiate everything to the benefit of the ranch."

"Yes," Gertrude said, taking a stitch into the quilt, "but then, he left here with much more than a long list."

The other women in the room fell silent. Jessica felt as though all eyes had turned on her to learn the truth. Swallowing her fear and pride, Jessica looked blankly at Mrs. Jenkins. "Yes, he also left with about one hundred head of prime steers."

Gertrude, not to be toyed with, smiled. "Yes, I suppose he'll be selling those for you in Kansas City."

"That's right."

The tension in the room mounted as Gertrude replied, "I suppose he'll be taking the money in cash."

Kate laughed. "Well, I certainly hope he doesn't take it in trade."

The other women chuckled. They appeared to know how Gertrude could be, as evidenced by the way they remained so obviously cautious at the first sign of her attack on Devon.

"I realize you believe the man can do no wrong," Gertrude said, continuing to focus her attention on Esther's quilt, "but you all know how I feel about him. You know how he hurt my Jane."

Unintelligible murmurings were the only response to this statement. Esther seemed to understand the pain it caused Jessica to hear such things. She smiled sweetly, giving Jessica the first sign of support from someone other than Kate.

"I believe the Carters to have raised a fine son," Esther began. "I knew his mother and father most of my life. When his father died and his mother and sister moved to Texas, I allowed him to stay here until he took up the position at Windridge. He showed only kindness and godliness while living in this house."

Gertrude was clearly offended by this and put down her sewing to stare angrily at Esther. "Are you suggesting that his actions with my daughter were kind and godly? Kissing another woman while only weeks away from marriage to another? No, Devon Carter is a deceiver. I only hope that his long absence doesn't signal yet another fault in him — that of theft."

"Devon is no thief!" Jessica declared, realizing how angry the woman had made her. "He has a job to do, and he will take as long as he needs in order to do it properly."

Gertrude turned a cold smile on Jessica. "Believe what you will, my dear, but actions have always spoken louder than words."

Jessica gripped the edge of her material so tightly that her fingers ached from the tension. Kate patted her gently, and Esther took up the cause. "Gerty, you'd do well to keep from being overly judgmental. You know what the Good Book says about such matters."

Gertrude appeared unfazed. "I know it says not to cast your pearls before swine. That's exactly what this naive young woman has done if she has given her fortune over to Devon Carter. If she has any expectations other than to find herself devoid of the money given over to that fool, then she's more naive than I think."

"I suppose the *Christian* thing to do," Esther suggested, "would be to pray for Devon's safe return."

Jessica felt like a lightning bolt had hit her. In all her worry and concern over Devon's whereabouts, she'd sorely neglected the one thing she could do to aid him. Pray. She'd fretted — given herself over to all manner of wild imaginings, talked about his absence — and now fought about it as well. But she'd not really prayed. Furthermore, she'd promised Devon that she would pray for him, and other than a quickly rattled off request for his health and safety, she'd not given the matter another thought.

"That's an excellent idea," Kate said. "Christian women should be more given over to speaking to God about matters rather than judging them falsely."

Gertrude glared at her, but Kate seemed unmoved by the obvious hostility that was directed at her.

From that point on, the day moved rather quickly. Jessica found herself actually enjoying the company of the women, in spite of the rather frustrating beginning to their day.

Later that afternoon, Esther stopped Jessica and Kate as they were preparing to leave. "Don't pay any mind to Gerty," she admonished. "The woman has a bitter heart. First, her daughter disgraces herself the way she did, then Gus refused her advances. She isn't likely to be a good friend to you, Jessica."

Jessica wanted to ask Esther about her father and Gertrude but decided it would make better conversation on the trip home with Kate. "Thank you for all you did," Jessica said instead. "I do appreciate it."

"That's what we older women do best," Esther said, patting Jessica's arm. "We have the privilege of not caring what others think about us because we're old enough to realize that the truth is more important than opinions. You stick with Kate, and she'll help you through this."

"I will," Jessica promised, already feeling much better.

"And one other thing," Esther added. "Your pa put a lot of faith in Devon Carter, and I put a lot of faith in your pa. He wasn't without his mistakes — sending you away after Naomi died was probably his biggest one. But he had a good heart, and he was smart as a whip. He could judge horseflesh and humans like no one I've ever known.

He trusted Devon for a reason." She paused and smiled. "The reason — Devon is worthy of trust. Plain and simple."

Jessica smiled and nodded. "Yes, he is."

Devon pulled up his coat collar in order to shield himself from the cold winter wind. It seemed the wind was worse in the city than in the Flint Hills. The tall buildings seemed to force the wind down narrow corridors and tunnels of roads and alleyways. He'd be glad to get home and knew he was long overdue. He'd thought to drop a postcard to Jessica and let her know about his delays, but always he figured he'd be leaving in a day or two at the most and would surely beat the thing to Windridge. What happened, however, was that one day turned into two and then into a week. And now Devon was clearly three weeks overdue and had sent no word to Jessica.

But there was a light at the end of the tunnel. Devon had finally managed to negotiate an order for the furniture needed at Windridge, and he'd arranged for the freighters to take the supplies out come spring. Then he'd taken it upon himself to telegraph his mother and ask her to speak on his behalf to Jeb Williams. This resulted in a telegram from Jeb himself stating he was more than happy to manage a deal between the Rocking W and Windridge. Devon felt as if he had the world by the tail. Everything was going better than he could have ever dreamed.

Now, as he made his way back to his hotel room, Devon decided the cold was a small price to pay. Tomorrow he would go to the train station, where he'd already made arrangements for those supplies he intended to take home with him, and board a train for home. How good it would be to see them all again. Especially Jessica and Ryan. He smiled at the thought of their birthday presents sitting back in his hotel room.

Kate had told him that both Jessica and Ryan shared their birthday with New Year's Eve. So along with baubles for Christmas, Devon had picked out toy soldiers for Ryan and a jewelry box for Jessica. He already imagined how he would place his grandmother's wedding ring inside the box and wait for her reaction when she realized that he was asking her to marry him. Turning down the alley where he always made his shortcut, Devon nearly laughed out loud. *She would be surprised to say the least,* he thought.

Halfway to the hotel, Devon felt the hair on the back of his neck prickle. He felt with certainty that someone had stepped into the alley behind him, but he didn't want to turn around and make a scene. He stepped up his pace but had gone no more than ten steps when a big burly man popped out from behind a stack of crates.

"I'll just be relieving you of your wallet," the man said in a surprisingly refined tone.

Devon felt a bit of relief, knowing that his wallet didn't contain much more than a few dollars. He'd secured his remaining money in the hotel safe, recognizing that it was foolish to walk about the city with large quantities of money.

He started to reach into his pocket just as the wind picked up. The gust came so strong that Devon's hat blew back off his head. He turned to catch it before it got away from him, but apparently the man who'd been following him took this as a sign of attack and struck Devon over the head.

Sinking to his knees, Devon fought for consciousness as the men began to beat him mercilessly. He thought of Jessica and how he wouldn't be leaving on the morning train. He thought of how worried she'd be when he didn't come back to Windridge. As his world went black, Devon Carter wondered if this was what it felt like to die.

CHAPTER 9

Christmas at Windridge came as a solemn affair. Jessica had no spirit for the holiday, and even Ryan moped about as though thoroughly discouraged at Devon having not returned. Kate and Buck had to admit that enough time had passed for Devon to have seen to all the responsibilities he'd gone to Kansas City in order to accomplish. They had very few words of encouragement for Jessica, and the house grew very quiet.

Jessica still tried to pray. She worried that Devon might lay ill somewhere in the city with no one to care for him. She fretted that he'd been unable to sell the cattle or that some other catastrophe had befallen him causing him to be unable to purchase the things they needed.

It was in a complete state of anxiety that Jessica decided to do a little cleaning. She started with Ryan's room, thoroughly scouring every nook and cranny in order to make certain it met with her approval. Then she started on her own room. She went through the closet, reorganizing her clothes and even managing to pull the feather tick and mattress from her bed in order to turn them. That was when she found her father's journal.

Surprised that a man like Gus Gussop had been given over to penning his thoughts onto paper, Jessica felt nervous about opening the book. She felt intrusive, almost as if she were committing some kind of sin. Her father had never shared any part of himself with her — at least not in the way Jessica had needed him to share.

Finding Ryan quite content to play in his room, Jessica took a seat near the fireplace and began to read.

" 'It's hard enough to allow my thoughts to come to mind,' " she read aloud, " 'but to put them to paper seems to give them life of their own.' "

These were the opening words of her father's journal. Eloquent speech for a rough-and-ready rancher who'd sent his only child away rather than be faced with raising her alone. Then Jessica had the startling realization that the words written here were to her mother.

Naomi, you should never have left me to face this alone. You knew I wouldn't be any good at it. You gave me a child, a beautiful daughter, and left me to live without you. How fair was that? I never had anything bad to say about you, with exception to this. You were wrong to go. Wrong to die and leave me here.

Jessica continued to read in silence, unable to speak aloud the words that followed.

She's beautiful, just like you. I can see it every time she comes to visit. I see you in the roundness of her face, the darkness of her brown eyes. I see you in her temperament when she gets a full head of steam up, and I hear you in her laughter. How I loved you, Naomi. How I love our little girl.

Jessica wiped away the tears that streamed down her face. Why couldn't he have told her these things? Why couldn't he have been honest with her and kept her at Windridge? The injustice of it all weighed heavily on her heart.

These long years have been like a death sentence to me, and the only reason I write these things now is that the doctor tells me I'll be joining you soon. What glory! To finally come home to you after all of these years. I know a man is supposed to look forward to heaven in order to be united with God, but forgive me, Lord, if I sin in this thought: It's Naomi I long to see.

Twenty-seven years is a long time to live without the woman you love. Others have tried to fill the void, but there is no one but you, my beloved. I tried to take interest in other women, but they paled compared to you, and how fair would it have been to have made another woman live here at Windridge in your shadow?

Jessica bit her lip to keep from sobbing out loud. Ryan would be very upset to see her cry, and with him just beyond the open doors of the nursery, she knew he'd hear her and come to investigate. The words of the journal opened an old wound that Jessica thought had healed with time. She felt the pain afresh, remembered the bitterness of leaving Windridge while her father watched from the porch — no wave, no kiss good-bye, no word.

She saw the devotion he held for her mother, believed that devotion extended in some strange way to herself, but also knew the emptiness her father had felt. An emptiness he imposed upon himself in order to be true to the memory of someone who had died nearly three decades ago.

It was never fair that I should have sent Jessica away from here. Kate scolded me daily for weeks, even months, and finally she stopped, seeing that I would not change my mind and bring the child home. I wanted to. Once Buck helped me past the worst of it, I wanted to bring Jess here to Windridge, but Harriet would have no part of it. We'd signed an agreement, which she so firmly reminded me of any-time I wrote to suggest doing otherwise.

Jessica startled at the realization that her father had tried to bring her back to her real home. She felt a growing anger at the knowledge that Aunt Harriet had kept her from such happiness. She thought of the years of strange girls' schools, where the loneliness threatened to eat her alive. She thought of her miserable youth and the par-ties and men who stood at Harriet's elbow, hoping to be chosen as a proper mate for Jessica. If only her father could have found a way to break the contract and bring her home. If only she had known that he desired her to be with him, she would have walked through fire to make it happen. She would have defied Harriet and all of her suitors in order to be back on Windridge permanently.

Naomi, I never imagined you would leave me. I built an empire to share with you. Built you a house on Windridge and planned a lifetime of happiness here in God's country. When you went away, you took all that with you. Took my hopes, my dreams, my future. After that, there was no one. Not even Jessica, because Harriet wouldn't allow her to be a part of my life.

Jessica could no longer contain her sobs. She moaned sorrowfully at the thought that her father had longed for her return.

Then Jessica married. He was nothing, less than nothing. A miserable worm handpicked by your aunt. I should have remembered her choice of husbands for you and realized how far I fell from the mark. How upset she was when you ran off with a cowboy from Kansas. Jessica had no one to fight for her, and she didn't have your strength of mind. She did what Harriet told her to do and married that eastern dandy who did nothing but bleed her dry.

Harriet died and left them a fortune, but Albright squandered it on gambling and women. I had him watched, knew his every move, but because Jess loved him, I did nothing. I couldn't hurt her more by interfering where I wasn't wanted. Devon Carter helped me to see that it was no longer my place to fret and stew. Devon's a good man. He's a Christian and a finer son a man could not ask to have. I consider him the son we never had. He's there, just two doors down, whenever I need him.

Jessica suddenly realized that Devon had lived in the house prior to her coming to Windridge. She also realized, without having to ask Kate for confirmation, that Devon had moved out of his own accord in order to maintain the proprieties for Jessica and Ryan. She'd only been coming for a visit as far as they had known. Her decision to stay had caused Devon to have to move permanently from the house. It made her feel bad to realize that she'd sent him off like the hired hand she'd so often accused him of being.

I've given Devon a piece of his own land, some two thousand acres on the south side. I also gave him a bonus of five thousand dollars. I figured if Gertrude Jenkins and Newman Albright could bleed me for funds, I might as well leave money to those I love. Jess will get the house, of course, and all of what remains of Windridge. Although in truth, I've neglected it badly, Naomi.

Several things came immediately to mind. First of all, Gertrude had taken money from her father, and from the sounds of it, she'd taken quite a bit. Jessica had known about Newman's indiscretions from her father's letters, but Gertrude came as a surprise.

But the most important thing that Jessica realized was that Devon Carter had his own money and his own land. He didn't need Jessica's pittance. He had no reason to run from Windridge and Kansas. He could have quit his position many times over and headed over to his own land and started a new life, but instead he stayed at Windridge — with her.

Warmth spread over Jessica in this revelation. Devon hadn't run away, taking her last dime. No, the delay was for some reason other than his alleged dishonesty, and with that thought, Jessica really began to worry. Perhaps he *had* fallen ill. Or maybe someone had done him harm. The possibilities were endless.

Wasting no more time with the diary, Jessica lovingly tucked the book beneath her pillow and went in search of Kate. There were several questions burning in her mind, and Kate would be the only one except Buck who could answer them.

Kate was in the kitchen mixing a cake when Jessica came bounding down the back stairs.

"Kate, I want the truth about something," Jessica announced.

Kate turned and looked at Jessica over the rim of her glasses. "As if I've ever given you anything else."

Jessica smiled. "I know you've been honest with me. That's why I know I can come to you now."

Kate seemed to realize the importance of the matter and put the mixing bowl aside. "So what's on your mind?"

"Devon."

"Now why doesn't that surprise me?"

Jessica smiled. "Devon lived here in the house when my father was alive, didn't he?"

Kate nodded. "How'd you find that out?"

"My father kept a journal shortly before he died. He knew he was dying and wrote the words as if speaking to my mother."

"I never knew this," Kate said in complete surprise. "Where did you find this journal?"

"Under my mattress," Jessica replied and laughed. "Remember how you wanted to turn the mattress last spring, and we only turned the tick and said we'd see to the mattress come fall? Well, I finally remembered it and took it on my own initiative to resolve the matter. When I managed to pull the mattress off, there it was."

"Well, I'll be," Kate said in complete amazement. "If I'd just turned that mattress after Gus died, we'd have found it a whole lot sooner. Guess that's what I get for being a poor housekeeper."

Jessica shook her head. "Don't you see? This was exactly as God intended it. There was a hardness to me when I came to Windridge that would never have allowed me to deal with the words I read in that journal. God knew the time was right and knew, too, that I needed to read those words."

"What words?"

"My father talked of how he loved me," Jessica said, tears forming anew in her eyes. "He talked, too, of how he loved Devon as a son. How he gave Devon land and money. Devon is considerably better off than I figured, isn't he?"

Kate smiled. "I don't know how much he has left. He took a good deal of his own money and started using it to fix up Windridge."

"What?"

"He knew he couldn't just offer it to you, Jess. He knew you'd say no. So he just started buying things that we needed. And he figured to add a good portion of his own funds to whatever the steers sold for and just tell you that he got a really good deal."

"And here I thought Devon was an honest man," Jessica said, wiping her eyes and smiling.

"He didn't want to hurt your feelings or spoil your dreams. Took a lot for him to accept the idea of a resort ranch, but he did it because he knew what it meant to you."

"I only wanted to make something of Windridge without relying on others for help. Guess that was my pride getting in the way of reality," Jessica admitted. "And to think I called Devon the hired help."

"That was pretty hard on him. Gus had treated him like a son, then you came along and relegated him to one of the hands."

Jessica shook her head. "Why didn't you tell me?"

"Devon made us promise we wouldn't. Made us promise we wouldn't say anything about any of it. As much as I love you, Jess, I couldn't betray that promise."

"Papa's diary also said that Gertrude Jenkins and my husband had bled him for money. What do you know about that?"

Kate thought for a moment. "I don't know too much about his dealings with Newman. I know your husband would send telegrams asking for money, telling of one emergency or another. Gus always sent whatever he asked for, knowing that even if Newman spent it on something other than what he claimed, it would at least keep you from suffering."

"It didn't keep me from suffering," Jessica replied. "But if Papa thought it did, then I'm glad."

"I think he knew the truth," Kate replied. "He knew about a lot we never gave him credit for. As for Gertrude, well, she thought she was going to talk Gus into marriage. She's a poor manager of that ranch of hers, and Gus lent her sum after sum, all in order to help her keep afloat. She finally deeded the ranch over to him, although no one was supposed to know that but she and Gus. That's part of the reason why she took off for Europe. She didn't want to face the retribution of listening to what folks would have to say when they learned she'd borrowed against the ranch until Gus owned the whole thing."

"Why wasn't I told about this?" Jessica asked.

Kate took a deep breath. "Because Devon arranged to buy the land from Gus, and when Gus died, Devon gave it back to Gertrude. It's the reason she hates him so much. He told her he knew he didn't owe her anything, but that he couldn't bear to see her suffer, especially if there was the slightest chance that he had somehow caused Jane to look elsewhere for her happiness. He also told her the truth about finding Jane in the arms of a traveling salesman. Told her how he confronted Jane, agreed to forget the whole matter, and still planned to marry her. It wasn't the story Gerty wanted to hear."

"I can well imagine."

"Anyway, Gus never knew. He probably figured Devon saw the merit of the property because it adjoined the land Gus had already given Devon."

Jessica wouldn't have thought it possible that she could love Devon more than she already did, but hearing of his generosity and giving to a woman who hated him made her realize how deeply she admired and loved Devon Carter.

"This changes everything," Jessica murmured, wishing silently that there might be a way to win Devon away from the woman he knew God had intended him to marry. *Perhaps that is the reason for his delay,* she thought for the first time. *Maybe he's gotten himself married.*

"Not really," Kate replied, interrupting Jessica's thoughts.

"What do you mean?" Jessica asked.

"You love him, and he loves you."

She shook her head sadly. "No, he told me there was someone he cared for. Someone God had chosen for him to marry."

Kate started laughing. "Silly woman, he meant you. He told Buck as much."

"What?" Jessica felt her chest tighten and her breathing quicken. "Are you telling me the truth?"

"I thought we'd already established that I've never lied to you. Do you think I'd start now?"

"No, but, I mean —" A wonderful rush of excitement flowed over Jessica. "He loves me?"

Kate laughed even more. "It's pretty obvious to everyone but you two that you're perfect for each other. You need each other in a bigger way than any two people I've ever seen. Whether you go back to regular ranching or run a resort, you'll do fine so long as you do it together."

"He loves me," Jessica repeated. "And he loves Ryan." She looked up at Kate and saw the happiness in the older woman's eyes. There was no doubting the words she spoke. Devon loved her.

Chapter 10

"Looks like it's gonna blow up a snow," Buck said, coming into the house. "I don't like the taste of the air. Wouldn't be surprised to see it shape up to be a bad one."

"Are we prepared for such a thing?" Kate asked.

"I'm having the boys bring up wood from the shed. We'll stack it high against the back of the house. That way, if we have a blizzard like the one the year Jessie was born, we won't have far to go for fuel."

"What about the hands?" Jessica asked, easily realizing the seriousness of the moment.

"They usually ride the storms out in the bunkhouse. We run a rope from there to the barns, and that way, they can keep an eye on the horses and milk cows."

Jessica nodded. "If it gets too bad, let's bring them up to the house. Better to use fuel to heat one place than two."

Buck and Kate exchanged a quick glance and smiled approvingly. "You sound more like your father each day," Kate told her.

Jessica laughed. "I would have thought that an insult at one time. Now, I take it as the compliment you intend it to be."

"I'll bring up extra fuel for the lanterns, and if you ladies think of anything else we need, you let me know," Buck said, heading back for the door. He opened it and looked outside. "Snow's already started," he announced.

"Then we'd best get busy," Kate told Jessica.

Ryan came into the kitchen about that time. His cheeks were flushed, and his eyes appeared rather glassy. Jessica immediately realized he'd been unusually quiet that morning. Picking up her son, Jessica could feel the heat radiating from his tiny body.

"Ryan's sick," she told Kate. "He has a fever."

Kate came to Jessica and held out her arms, but Jessica felt all her feelings of overprotection and inadequacy surface. "I'll take care of him," she said more harshly than she'd intended.

Kate nodded as if understanding. "I only wanted to see how high his fever was."

"You can tell by a touch?" Jessica asked,

214

still clinging tightly to Ryan.

"You can when you've dealt with as many sick boys as I have. Remember, I've nursed the bunk hands, my own sons, Gus, and Buck, even Devon. You get a feel for it after a time." Kate put her hand to Ryan's head. "Feels pretty high. We'd best get him to bed and see what we can do to bring that fever down. Do you see any rashes on his body?"

"Rashes?" Jessica asked in a panicky voice.

Kate nodded. "I heard some of the New-come kids were down with the measles."

"Measles!" Jessica's voice squeaked out the word. "He just can't have measles."

"Well only time will tell. Let's get him to bed, and we'll work on it from there. Why don't you put him in the bed in our room? That way you won't have to run up and down the stairs all the time, and it'll be warmer here by the kitchen. If you like, you can sleep there, and Buck and I will take one of the upstairs rooms."

"Thanks, Kate." Jessica looked down at Ryan, who had put his head on her shoulder. It was so uncharacteristic of the boy that Jessica thought she might start to cry. She bit her lower lip and, knowing nothing else to do, began to pray.

The blizzard blew in with the full force

Buck had expected and then some. Icy pellets of rain came first, coating everything with a thick layer of ice. Then sleetlike snow stormed across the hills, and visibility became impossible.

Jessica thought very little about the storm, except to occasionally worry about Devon. She had far too much with which to concern herself by keeping on top of Ryan's needs and easily relegated everything else to Buck and Kate.

By the second day of the storm, Ryan bore the telltale signs of measles. Tiny red splotchy dots covered his stomach and groin, and his fever refused to abate. Jessica found herself so weary she could hardly keep her eyes open, yet when Kate offered to relieve her, Jessica refused.

"You aren't doing yourself or Ryan any good," Kate told her. "I don't know why you can't see the sense in letting others help you." Kate's tone revealed the offense she took at Jessica's actions.

"I'm sorry, Kate. I didn't mean to make you feel bad. It's just that . . . well . . . he's mine, and it's my responsibility to see him through this."

"But if you kill yourself trying to nurse him back to health, what good will it do? I swear, the way you act, you'd think I was trying to steal your glory."

"What?" Jessica questioned, struggling to clear the cobwebs from her sleepy mind. "What glory is there in a sick child?"

"None that I know of," Kate replied. "But you seem to think there's some reason to keep anyone else from getting too close to that boy."

Jessica slumped into a chair and nodded. "I just can't lose him. He's so important to me. I don't want to lose him to you or Devon or sickness."

"Why would you lose him to anyone? Ryan knows you're his mother, and he loves you. Well, as much as any two year old can love. Jessica," Kate said, reaching out to touch the younger woman's shoulder, "you've been like a daughter to me. I always wanted to have a daughter, and I would have happily raised you for Gus. Let me offer you a bit of motherly advice."

Jessica looked up and nodded.

"Don't let fear be the glue that binds your relationship with Ryan. Fear is a poor substitute for love."

"But you know about the past. You know what Essie did when I lived in New York."

"Yes, but I don't see Essie around here. It's just you and me, and I'm not about to steal your child away from you. Don't you see, Jessica? The more you smother Ryan with protectiveness and isolate him from being able to love anyone but you, the more hollow and useless your relationship. He'll run the first chance he gets, just to give himself some breathing room."

"I know you're right. God's been working on this very issue with me. I guess I just let fear control me sometimes."

"Sometimes?" Kate questioned with a grin.

"All right, so fear and I are no strangers," Jessica said, smiling. "Kate, would you please watch Ryan while I get some sleep?"

Kate nodded and patted Jessica once again. "I would be happy to help."

Jessica nodded, made her way to the bed, and fell across it, not even bothering to undress.

Father, she prayed, *please heal my son. You know how much I love him and how lost I would be without him. I'm begging You not to take him from me.*

She felt welcome drowsiness engulf her. Devon's face came to mind and, with it, the thought that she needed to pray for him. *Watch over him, Father,* she added. *Please bring him home to Windridge.*

The snow let up, but not the wind, which kept the effects of the blizzard going on for

218

days. The blowing snow blinded them from even seeing the top of Windridge. Jessica saw notable improvements in Ryan's health and forced herself to accept Kate's involvement in nursing him. It wasn't that she didn't dearly love Kate, but the fact was, Jessica still needed to let go of her possessive nature when it came to the boy.

Sitting at her father's desk in the library, Jessica thought back on the things Devon, Kate, and Buck had told her over the course of her time at Windridge.

"Folks need folks out here," Buck had once said. *"It fast becomes a matter of survival."* His point had been made in talking to her about selling property to Joe Riley. He needed a spring in order to assure himself of having water for his cattle and his land. Jessica could easily see that what Buck said made perfect sense. They were so isolated out here in the middle of the Flint Hills that to be anything other than neighborly could prove fatal.

She stared into the fireplace and watched the flames lick greedily at the dry wood. Kate had said, *"It's better to rely on folks than to die on folks."* This was kind of an unspoken code of Kate's. *"The prairie is no place for pride,"* Kate had added. *"Pride not only goeth before destruction, it is the thing that stirs up strife and causes heartache."*

Jessica knew it was true. Her own pride had nearly caused her to alienate Kate's affections. That was something she could never have abided. Kate was like a mother to her in so many ways that Aunt Harriet had never been. Aunt Harriet had raised her, but Aunt Harriet had never loved her the way Kate did.

Devon came to mind when Jessica thought about love. She loved him so much that it hurt to think about what tragedies might have befallen him. She planned to have Buck go into town and wire the livestock yards in Kansas City. They would have records of the cattle transactions and just possibly those records would include the name of the hotel where Devon was staying. It was Jessica's hope that they might learn something about Devon's whereabouts by starting down this path.

But the blizzard had put an end to that thought, and Buck felt certain more snow was coming their way. She felt her enthusiasm slip another notch. Life on the prairie was very hard — there could be no doubt about that — and it was quickly becoming apparent that Jessica could either accept that she could do nothing on her own, or she could perish.

"Don't be so sure you don't need anyone," Devon had told her once. It had startled her to have him read her so easily. She smiled when she thought of the halfhearted protest she'd offered him. She could still see the laughter in his eyes and the amusement in his voice when she'd told him he didn't know anything about her feelings.

"I may not know you or your feelings," he'd countered, *"but I know pride when I see it. Pride used to be a bosom companion of mine, so I feel pretty certain when I see him. Just remember, pride isn't the kind to stick around and help when matters get tough."*

Jessica chuckled at the memory. *He's so right,* she thought. *Pride only offers seclusion and a false sense of security. I have to let go of my pride and allow people to help me when I need it and to help others when they have needs. Otherwise, Ryan and I will never survive life at Windridge.*

"It's been two weeks," Devon heard someone say. His mind was lost in a haze of darkness, but from time to time someone spoke words that made a little sense. He strained to understand the words — fought to find the source of the words.

"His vital signs are good, but the fact that

he's still not regained consciousness worries me."

"Any word on the man's identity?" came another male voice.

"None. We really should send someone around to contact the businesses in the area where he was found."

Devon floated on air and wondered why everyone seemed so concerned. Who was this person they couldn't identify, and what were vital signs?

"His injuries were extensive," the man continued, "but the bones seem to be healing just fine, and the swelling has gone down in his face. It's probably that blow to the back of the head that keeps him unconscious."

From somewhere in his thoughts, Devon began to realize they were talking about him. It startled him at first, but then it seemed quite logical. The next realization he had was of being in extreme pain. Something wasn't right. Somewhere in his body, someone was causing him a great deal of torment.

These thoughts came and went from time to time, but to Devon they seemed to transpire in the course of just a few hours. It wasn't until he heard one of the disembodied voices announce that if he didn't regain consciousness soon, he would die, that Devon began a long hard fight to find his way through the mire of blackness.

"Did you have a nice Christmas?" someone questioned.

"A very nice one, sir," came the feminine voice in response.

Devon thought for a moment the voice belonged to someone he knew, but the thought was so fleeting that he couldn't force it to stay long enough to interpret it.

"The New Year's ball was superb," the woman continued. "I'd never been to anything so lovely."

"Yes, my wife loves the occasion. Of course, it's also her birthday," the man responded.

Birthday. Devon thought about the word for a moment. Someone he knew had a birthday on New Year's Eve. Without realizing what he was doing, Devon opened his eyes and said, "Birthday."

His eyes refused to focus for several minutes, but when they did, Devon could see the startled faces of the man and woman who stood at his bedside.

"So, you finally decided to join the world of the living," the man said in a stern voice that was clearly mingled with excitement.

"Where am I?" Devon asked, his voice

gravelly.

"You're in the hospital. Have been for nearly a month," the man replied. "I'm Dr. Casper, and you are?"

He waited for Devon's response with a look of anticipation. The woman, too, looked down at him in an expectant manner. Devon stared blankly at them, trading glances first with the woman and then with the man.

"Did you understand my question?" the doctor asked. "I need to know who you are."

"I don't know," Devon replied with a hideous sinking feeling. He shook his head, feeling the dull pain that crossed from one side of his skull to the other. "I don't know who I am."

CHAPTER 11

The weeks that followed left Devon depressed and frustrated. His injuries were quick enough to heal, so why not his mind? "How does that leg feel?" the doctor questioned as Devon hobbled around the room like a trained monkey.

"It's sore, but I've had worse."

"How do you know?" the doctor asked curiously. "Are you starting to remember something more?"

Devon shrugged. "I remember little pieces of things. I remember a room with a stone fireplace. I remember riding a horse out on the open range." He hobbled back to bed and sunk onto the edge of the mattress. "But I don't remember anything important."

"Those things are all important, Mr. Smith," the doctor told him.

"Don't call me Smith," Devon replied angrily. "Not unless you have proof that

that's who I am."

"We have to call you something," the doctor replied. "Now, raise that arm for me."

Devon lifted his left arm and grimaced. Apparently his assailants had hit him repeatedly and kicked him as well. He had suffered busted ribs, a broken ankle, and a dislocated shoulder. His left arm had been continuously pounded, the doctor believed by boot heels, as had his face.

"It still works. Just not as well," Devon told the doctor.

"I'm sure in time it will all heal properly. Are you in as much pain today as you were yesterday?"

Devon shook his head. "No." He glanced up to find one of the nurses coming down the ward with a well-dressed man at her side.

"Dr. Casper, this man believes he knows our patient."

Devon perked up at this and studied the man for a moment. Was he a friend? A brother? Some other family member?

"Yes," the man said enthusiastically. "This is the man I've been searching for. He didn't have a beard when he stayed with us, but he's the same man. He's a guest, or was a guest, at our hotel. I'm so happy to have found you, Mr. Carter."

"Carter?" Devon tried the name. Carter. Yes, Carter sounded right.

"The assault this man received left him without much of a memory," Dr. Casper told the hotelman.

"No wonder you failed to return," the man said sympathetically. "When I heard about the poor man who'd been beaten in the alley not far from the hotel, I thought, perhaps this is Devon Carter. I knew you wouldn't leave without retrieving your things. After all, you left quite a bit of money in my safe."

Devon nodded. Yes, he remembered having a good amount of money. He closed his eyes and pictured himself handing it over to the man who now stood at his side. "I remember you."

"Good," the doctor said enthusiastically. "Seeing something familiar often triggers memory." He turned to the hotelman. "Did you bring any of his things?"

"No, but I can have them brought here immediately."

"Then do so," the doctor instructed. "Mr. Carter will need all the help he can get in order to remember who he is."

Nearly half an hour later, a boy appeared with saddlebags, two brown paper packages, and a large envelope. The man from the hotel stood at his side as though standing guard. "We have your things, Mr. Carter."

Devon nodded. It felt so good just to know his own name that knowing anything else would be purely extra. He took hold of the saddlebags and noted the carved initials *D.C.* He ran his fingers over the indentation, remembering vaguely the day he'd carved the marker on the bags. Reaching into one side, Devon pulled out his shaving gear and studied it for a moment. It seemed familiar, but nothing that offered him any real memory. Next, he took out an extra shirt and pair of socks. Nothing came to mind with those articles, so he quickly reached into the other side of the bag.

Here, he found receipts all dated from the middle of December. Some of the receipts were for furniture, and others were for homey things like lamps, curtain rods, material, dishes, and such. The kind of things a wife would have need and desire of. Did he have a wife? The same face kept coming to mind. At first she had appeared only in a hazy outline, but as time went on, the warmth of her smile and the sincerity in her dark eyes became clearer in his memory. Was this the image of his wife?

"Do you remember these things?" the doctor questioned.

"Somewhat," Devon replied.

"This," the man from the hotel said, "is the money you left with us."

Devon took the envelope and looked inside. There was a great deal of money, and it immediately triggered a thought. The money was intended for a special use. The money belonged to her. The woman in his mind. Perhaps it was a dowry. Maybe they were setting up house, and this money had come from her.

"Why don't you unwrap these packages? My nurse will be glad to rewrap them afterward, but perhaps they will trigger some memory."

Devon nodded and gently stripped away the paper on the first package. Toy soldiers. Devon felt mounting frustration at not being able to remember. Then to his surprise, the image of another face came to mind. It was that of a child. The fuzzy brown hair of the boy seemed to draw Devon's attention first. There was something important about this child. Then a horrible feeling washed over Devon. Was he not only a husband but a father as well?

"Here, try this one," the doctor said, helping to pull the paper from the other package. A jewelry box was revealed as the paper fell away. Devon stared at the box, feeling sure that he should remember it but having no real understanding of why. Had he bought this as a gift for the woman in his dreams? Had he left a family somewhere to worry and fret over his well-being? What if they were in danger because of his absence? What if they needed the supplies and goods he had procured?

"No," he muttered, handing the things over to the nurse. He stuffed the receipts and money into the saddlebag, then turned to the hotelman. "I don't suppose I gave you an address?"

"No sir, but you said you were from Kansas. You came to sell cattle."

Devon drew his legs up onto the bed and fell back against the pillow. "I think I need to rest," he told them all. He felt angry and frustrated. He had hoped that with the recognition of his own name, he might instantly remember everything else that he needed to know.

"Thanks for bringing my things," he told the hotelman. The man smiled and prodded the kid to follow him from the room. The nurse and doctor agreed that rest was the best solution and finally left Devon alone.

He stared at the ceiling for a while, then rolled onto his side and stared down the corridor of beds. Several men moaned and called out for help. Others slept peacefully, and a few read. But all of them had their minds. All of them knew their name and recognized their own things.

Sleep finally overtook Devon, and although he passed the time fitfully, he actually felt better when he awoke. The light had faded outside, leaving little doubt that dusk was upon them. This time of day made Devon melancholy. He longed to be home — wherever home might be.

He thought of the dark-haired woman in his dreams. Thought of the child whose laughing face warmed his heart. He loved these people; he felt certain of that. They were important to him in a way he couldn't figure out, but he knew without a doubt they were keys to his past.

Supper came, and although Devon had figured nothing good could come of the meal, he found himself actually enjoying the beef stew. It wasn't as good as Kate's, but . . .

Kate? Was that the dark-haired woman's name?

Devon stared at the stew and forced an image. He was sitting in a stylish dining room. The dark-haired woman and little boy were sitting beside him, but there was also someone else in the picture. An older woman's face beamed a smile at him. She pushed up wire-rimmed glasses and asked if he'd like more stew. *Kate. Katie!* He actually remembered her.

This triggered other thoughts, and soon Devon found himself overwhelmed with people and events. Still, he couldn't remember the brown-haired woman's name, nor that of the child. Nor could he remember where he lived and where he might find the others.

"I've brought another visitor," Dr. Casper said as he approached Devon's bed.

The supper had grown cold, but Devon didn't care. "I've been remembering some things."

The doctor smiled. "Good! That's very good. This gentleman called for you at the hotel, and he knows quite a bit about your home. We thought you might remember him as well."

Devon looked at the man and nodded. "Yes, he does seem familiar."

"I am Mr. Whitehead. You ordered a large number of chairs and two bedsteads from my company. You also ordered several nightstands and dressers." The man chuckled. "You look a bit different what with the beard. You had the mustache, but the beard is new."

Devon nodded and smirked a grin. "Nobody seems to offer me a shave around here. You say I ordered furniture? I do seem to remember something along those lines, but did I say why I needed so much?"

"You were ordering them for your place in Kansas. You are planning a resort ranch at a place called Windridge."

The word *Windridge* triggered everything. Suddenly it was as if the floodgates to his mind had opened. He realized exactly who he was and who she was. "Jessica." He breathed the name and sighed.

Then, startling both the doctor and Mr. Whitehead, Devon exclaimed, "What day is this?"

"February 3," the doctor replied.

Devon rubbed his bearded face. "Get me a razor and some soap. I have to get home. I should have been there months ago."

The doctor smiled. "Are you certain you feel up to leaving us?"

Devon nodded. "I'm positive. Just get me my things. Oh, and I need to send a telegram." No doubt everyone would be worried sick by now. Especially Jessica.

"Well, it seems as though this is all working out rather well," Dr. Casper said. "I wouldn't have given you odds on pulling through that beating, but you're one tough man, Mr. Carter."

"I don't know about how tough I am, but I'm definitely a man with a purpose, and that gives a guy strength, even when all hope is lost."

When they left him to dress, Devon felt the overwhelming urge to get down on his knees and thank God for supplying him with the answers he'd been so desperately seeking. Stiff and sore from his inactivity, Devon ignored the pain and knelt beside his bed.

Thank You, Father, he prayed, feeling hot tears come to his eyes. *I was so lost, and I despaired of ever being found. But You knew where I was all the time. You knew what I needed, and You brought it to me. I pray with a heart of thanksgiving for all that You've done to rescue me from the hopelessness. Please keep Jessica and everyone at Windridge in Your care. Help them not to worry, and help me to get home to them quickly. Amen.*

Jessica awoke with a start. She went first to Ryan's bed and found the boy sleeping peacefully. All signs of the measles were gone, but he was still rather weak, and Jessica worried over him.

She watched him sleep peacefully and thanked God for His mercy.

"I've learned so much here at Windridge," she murmured. "Things I never expected to learn."

She thought of the diary her father had kept and went to take it up from the special place she'd given it on her fireplace mantel. Lighting a lamp, she sat down to reread the final entry in the journal. She continued to come back to this one entry, because while the rest of the book was written to her mother, this entry was written to her:

My beloved Jessica,

I can only pray that you will someday forgive me for sending you away. I have always loved you, will die loving you, but I know I am unworthy of your love. I've tried to help out where I could — tried to be there for you when you would let me, which, although it didn't happen often, happened just enough to give me some satisfaction.

Please know this, I never blamed you for your mother's passing. People live, and people die, and that's just the way things are. Only God chooses the timing for those things. Only God can give life, as He did in the form of my beautiful child, and only God can take life, as He did with your mother.

I'm sorry I can't leave you a legacy of memories spent here at Windridge, but I hope you'll stay on. I hope you'll come to love this house as much as your mother did. I hope, too, that you'll be good to Katie and Buck and Devon Carter. You don't know any of them very well, but they're good people, and I know they will care very deeply for you. When you think of me, Jessica, I hope it will be with something other than hatred and anger. Maybe one day you will actually think of me as I used to be when your mother was alive. Hopeful, happy, looking forward to the future and all that it had to offer.

Your Father

Jessica sighed and closed the book to cradle it against her breast. She felt warmed and comforted by its words. Now if only Devon would come home. If only they could have some word from him. Some hope that he was all right.

Getting up, Jessica walked to the window and looked across the snowy prairie. "Come home to me, Devon," she whispered against the frosty glass. "Please come home to Windridge."

CHAPTER 12

Warm southerly winds blew in and melted the snows on Windridge. The land went from white to dull brown practically overnight. Jessica marveled at the change. She could actually go outside without a coat, although Kate told her the warmth was deceptive. But Jessica didn't care. The heat of the sun felt good upon her face, and the warm winds blowing across the land would dry the ground and insure her ability to get to town again.

Jessica didn't allow herself to be concerned with what she would do once she actually got to town. She hadn't a clue as to how she would go about searching for Devon, but she knew the key would be in communication. She would start by telegraphing anyone who might have some idea of Devon's whereabouts.

Bundling Ryan up, Jessica decided a walk to the top of the ridge would be in order.

The land was still rather soggy, but Jessica carefully picked her way up the hill while Ryan chattered about the things he saw.

"Bword," he cried out, pointing to a robin sitting on the fence post.

"Yes, that's a good sign," Jessica told her son.

"I want bword," Ryan said, trying to squirm out of her hold.

"No. Now stop it," Jessica reprimanded. "We're going up here to see if we can find Devon."

"Dadon," Ryan repeated.

Jessica smiled. No matter how much Ryan's language improved, Devon's name still came out sounding like some form of *Daddy.*

"Dadon comin'," Ryan said enthusiastically.

"Soon, I hope." Jessica wondered if she'd made a mistake by telling the boy they were looking for Devon. Now he would be constantly chattering about Devon, always asking where he was and when he'd come home. The measles had forced all of them to focus their attention on something other than Devon's absence, and even though Ryan had cried for Devon on more than one occasion, he seemed to accept that the man was gone from his life. At least temporarily.

Now Jessica realized she'd probably stirred up the child's anticipation all over again.

"Dadon comin' to me," Ryan told her, patting his hand against her face.

Jessica kissed his fingers and laughed. "I pray he comes home soon." She trudged up the final few feet of the ridge, realizing as she did how much Ryan had grown since the last time she'd carried him up the hillside.

"Oh Ryan," she said rather breathlessly, "you're getting so big."

"Wyan get big," he said, raising his arms high in the air. "Dadon comin' to me."

Jessica shook her head and grinned at the boy's enthusiasm. *Let him have his moment,* she thought. *It can't hurt to be hopeful.* Jessica stared out across the Flint Hills and felt the longing in her heart grow stronger. He was out there somewhere.

"I don't know where you are," she whispered, her skirts bellowing out behind her as the wind whipped at them. She knew she couldn't keep Ryan outside for much longer and had just started to turn back down the hill when she spotted a wagon emerge from behind a hill.

Ryan saw the object as well and started clapping his hands. "Dadon comin'!"

Jessica felt her heart skip a beat as yet

another wagon followed the first and then another. Four wagons in all, laden with crates and covered boxes, made their way toward Windridge. Then Jessica caught the outline of the two men in the lead wagon.

"Devon," she whispered, feeling absolutely confident that the man beside the driver of the wagon was her beloved Devon.

"Come on, Ryan, we have to get you back in the house."

"I want Dadon," Ryan protested as Jessica nearly ran down the hill.

Because the grass still held moisture, she slipped and nearly fell. "I've got to calm myself down," she said aloud and forced herself to walk more carefully.

Seeing the wagons come ever closer, Jessica forgot about taking Ryan inside. She forgot about everything but getting to Devon. She started walking down the dirt road, her pace picking up as the wagons rounded the final bend. She tightened her grip on Ryan. *Devon's home!* It was all she could think of.

He apparently saw her, because the wagon stopped long enough for Devon to jump down from the seat. He waved the driver on and walked toward them with a bit of a limp. *He was hurt!* she thought, and all sensibility left her mind. She began to run, mindless of Ryan, mindless of the drivers passing by in their wagons.

"Oh Devon!" she exclaimed. His face registered surprise as she crossed the final distance and threw herself into his arms. "Oh Devon, I thought you were never coming home." Then without thought, she kissed him. At first it was just a peck on the cheek, then another and another, and finally her lips met his and stopped. All rational thought had fled, and she kissed him passionately. Pulling away, Jessica suddenly realized by the look on Devon's face that she'd made a grave mistake.

Her enthusiasm waned, in spite of the fact that Ryan was now clapping and shouting Devon's name over and over. She did nothing for a moment, her gaze fixed on Devon. She searched his eyes for some sign of acceptance, but he only stared back at her as if trying to figure out who she was and why she'd just kissed him.

Thrusting Ryan into Devon's arms, Jessica turned and ran back to the house. He didn't even call after her. Jessica felt her face grow hot with humiliation. Kate must have been wrong about his feelings for her. She must have misunderstood Buck, or Buck had misunderstood Devon.

Jessica wanted to die. Wanted to crawl

under a rock and never be seen again. What a spectacle she'd just made of herself. Running out there to Devon as though he was her long lost love.

But, she thought, *he is* my *love.* She might not be his, but he was her own heart's love. And deep down inside, Jessica knew she would never love another. If he couldn't return that love, then she would live the rest of her life alone. The thought terrified her.

"Is that Devon?" Kate exclaimed, stepping out the front door.

"Yes," Jessica barely managed to say. She rushed past, mindless of the shocked expression on the older woman's face. She couldn't stand and explain her humiliating actions to Kate. No, let Devon tell Kate how poorly she'd conducted herself.

Jessica stayed out of sight until suppertime. Kate had brought Ryan to the nursery for his nap, and although Jessica was just in the adjoining room, she didn't open the doors to speak to the woman; Kate, thankfully, didn't knock and ask her to.

She felt guilty for having neglected Ryan, but in truth her emotions were so raw and foreign that Jessica knew it would have been impossible to deal with anyone.

"I don't know what to do," she whispered,

pressing her face against the cool pane of the window. "I made a fool of myself, and now I have to face them all at supper."

She heard Kate ring the supper bell, something the woman had come up with in order to call guests to meals. The tradition had been started early, all in order to see how and if it would work. The bell pealed out loud and clear, and Jessica cringed. She would have to go down. There was no other way.

She splashed water on her face and checked her appearance. She'd changed out of the skirt and blouse she'd worn earlier. The hem of that skirt had been laden with mud and grass, and the blouse had clung to her from perspiration. Now she studied her reflection and realized that the peach-colored gown made her look quite striking. The muttonleg sleeves made her shoulders look slightly wider, which accented her tiny waist. The gown was cut in a very simple style, with a rounded neckline and basque waist. The peach material had been trimmed in cream-colored lace and cording, and with Jessica's brunette hair, the effect was quite stunning.

She bit her lip and shook her head. It didn't matter. She had dressed for him, but it wouldn't matter. His feelings had obviously changed while he'd been away from Windridge. She would have to accept this fact and deal with her broken heart.

"Mama! Mama come!" Ryan called out to her from the nursery.

Jessica smiled and opened the door. "Yes, Mama is coming."

By the time they made their way into the dining room, the others had already congregated. Jessica hated making an entrance where everyone could stare at her, but she knew there was no other choice. She swept into the room, Ryan in her arms, and made her way to the table determined that no one would think anything was wrong.

"Here we are. So sorry for the delay," she announced, putting Ryan in his chair and taking her own place at the foot of the table.

"I thought perhaps you'd fallen asleep," Kate said, allowing Buck to help her into her chair.

Jessica could feel Devon's gaze upon her, but she refused to look at him. "Yes, well, I did rest for a time. Thank you for seeing to Ryan."

"Oh, I didn't see to him except to put him down for his nap. Devon wouldn't hear of it. He insisted that they had a lot of catching up to do."

Jessica could feel her cheeks grow warm.

"Well, then, thank you." She refused to say his name. It was almost more than she could stand. Being so near to him yet knowing that he was put off at her behavior was too much to bear.

They blessed the meal, with Buck giving thanks for Devon's safe return. Then Kate started the conversation, asking Devon to explain his long absence.

"As I was telling Buck and Kate earlier," Devon began, "everything went pretty well the first couple weeks. I had no trouble selling the cattle and arranging for most everything we had on our list."

Our list. The words sounded pleasant, but Jessica knew she could take no comfort in them. Devon merely thought of Windridge as being partly his own because her father had instilled that belief in the man. How could she blame him for his concerns about the ranch and what would become of it?

"They hit me hard and of course —"

"What?" Jessica nearly shouted, and for the first time her gaze met his. "Who hit you?"

Devon grinned. "I was just telling you that I got myself mugged in Kansas City. A couple fellows waylaid me in the alley not far from the hotel. Thankfully, the money was secured in the hotel safe, and those thugs only managed to get about five dollars. But they hit me hard on the back of the head, then proceeded to beat me. They thought they'd killed me, and why not? I was unconscious and bloodied up pretty good."

Jessica could only stare at him. Her throat tightened as if a band had been tightly wrapped around her neck.

"By leaving me for dead, they did me a favor. Someone found me and hauled me off to the hospital. I was in a coma for about three weeks."

"A coma." Jessica barely breathed the words.

Devon nodded. Ryan began calling for something to eat, and Devon reached over to hand the boy a piece of bread without stopping his story. "When I woke up, I hurt like all get out, but the worst of it was that I couldn't remember a thing."

"Nothing?" Jessica questioned.

His eyes seemed to darken as they locked with hers. "Nothing. I didn't know who I was or where I was from. I only knew the pain and misery of my condition. I couldn't even tell the police what had happened."

"But God was watching over you," Kate chimed in. "We've been praying for you. When you didn't turn up by Christmas, we all had a feeling something wasn't quite right."

"Especially given that you didn't even bother to send a telegram," Buck added.

Devon pulled a wrinkled piece of paper from his pocket. It was clearly a telegram, and he unfolded it and held it up. "I found this waiting at the telegraph office. I sent this as soon as I had my memory back. Seems you people have been impossible to get to because of the snow."

Buck laughed. "That we were, but you could have let us know sooner."

"I know. I should have, but I kept thinking that I'd be coming home any day. Then one week's delay turned into two and so on, and then they mugged me, and well, now you know the story."

"But what happened to help you regain your memory?" Jessica asked.

"A fellow from the hotel came around to see me. He'd heard about the mugging, and since I never returned for the money in the safe, he thought it might be me. He brought some of my things, and little bits of memory started coming back. Then one of the vendors with whom I'd set up a purchase order for chairs came to the hotel when I never came back around to see him. He learned about my situation and came to see me at the hospital, and he was able to help me put together the rest of the mystery."

"What an awful time, Devon," Kate said shaking her head. "I just don't know how a fellow could manage without his memories."

"It was hard. I knew there was so much waiting for me, but I just couldn't force it to come to mind."

Jessica shook her head. "How very awful."

"Well, it's behind us now. I have a bit of limp from a broken ankle, and my ribs still hurt me a bit, but my hard head kept them from doing me in."

Buck laughed. "As many times as you've been thrown from one green horse or another, I'd say that head of yours has held up pretty well."

They all laughed at this. All but Jessica. She pretended to busy herself with preparing Ryan's food. The boy was growing bored with bread, and it was clear he felt himself entitled to something more. She thanked God silently for bringing Devon home to them. She couldn't imagine why such a thing had been necessary to endure, yet Kate had assured her that all things happened for a purpose. As if reading her mind, Devon spoke up again.

"Being laid up like that made me realize just how much I still wanted to accomplish.

It made me realize how important some things were and how unimportant other things were."

"How so, Devon?" Kate asked, ladling him a large portion of the beef stew he'd specifically requested for supper.

"I realized it doesn't much matter what direction we go with Windridge so long as we're happy and doing what God would have us do. What does matter is that we honor God and care for one another. Everything else is just icing on the cake."

"Cake. Wyan want cake!"

Devon laughed and rubbed the boy's head. "I do believe this boy grew some hair while I was gone." Ryan squealed and clapped his hands as if acknowledging his own accomplishments.

Jessica thought about what Devon had said long after the supper meal was over and Ryan had been put to bed. She had thought to just stay in her room, but at the sound of the bell ringing downstairs, she figured Kate had forgotten something and was using the signal to keep from having to trudge up a flight of steps to get her answer.

With a sigh, Jessica went down the back stairs to the kitchen and found Devon leaning casually against the wall at the bottom of the stairs — bell in hand, grin on his face.

"I wondered if this would really work. Kate said it would, but I just didn't believe her."

Jessica began to tremble. She froze on the step and waited to see what he would do or say next. His smile broadened as he set the bell aside. "I thought maybe you'd take a walk with me. Kate says she'll listen for Ryan, so why don't you grab up your coat and come out to the ridge with me?"

Jessica felt her mouth go dry. "I don't know if that's such a good idea."

Devon laughed and reached up to pull her down the last few steps. "Well I do. The country air seems to have a remarkable effect on you."

Jessica's face grew hot. Was he implying what she thought he was? She didn't get a chance to ask because he moved her toward the back door with such speed that she had no time to protest.

He pulled her work coat from the peg and helped her on with it. Then he took up his own coat, which he'd draped haphazardly atop the butter churn. "Come on."

He half dragged her up the hill, not saying a word as they made their way to the top. Jessica felt the warmth of his fingers intertwined with her own. It felt wonderful to have him so near. But how could she ever explain her actions from earlier in the day? No doubt he wanted to discuss her boldness, and he probably wanted to upbraid her for it, given the fact that he was taking her away from the house and other listening ears.

She bit at her lower lip and tried to think of how she would justify herself. She'd simply tell him she was overcome with joy. Which was true. Then, she'd make it clear the kiss meant nothing. Which was not true.

Devon slowed down as they neared the top and nearly swung her in a circle as they came to stand atop the ridge. "Now," he said without wasting any time. "I'd like an explanation."

"An explanation?" Jessica questioned, barely able to look him in the eye. "For what?"

The full moon overhead revealed the amusement in his expression. "All the time you've been here at Windridge, Jessica Albright, you've either been putting me in my place, arguing with me about how things would be, or calling me the hired help. You've berated me for my interference with Ryan, refusing to let him get too close for fear I might steal him away from you, and you've hidden yourself away anytime things got too uncomfortable."

Jessica said nothing. Everything he'd related was true. It hardly seemed productive to deny it.

"Then," he said, his voice lowering, "I return home from an experience that nearly sent me to my maker, and you greet me like I'm your long lost husband. And that, my dear Jessica, is what I want an explanation for."

Jessica took a deep breath. Her moment of truth had come. But she couldn't tell him the truth, not given the way he'd reacted to her. Or could she? Maybe if she was honest, he'd realize the merit in accepting her love. Maybe he'd even come to love her the way Kate presumed he already did.

The air had grown chilly, and Jessica shivered. She refused to give in to her fears. Her entire life had been a pattern of running away from painful situations, and while she'd not instigated the first time when her father had sent her from Windridge, she had certainly allowed many of the other situations.

"Well?" Devon prodded.

His expression was unreadable. Where earlier Devon had smiled with amusement and seemed quite entertained by her nervousness, Jessica could find nothing in his face to reveal how he really felt. She would have to swallow her pride and admit her feelings or lie to him.

"I suppose you do deserve an explanation," she began slowly. "I can best explain by telling you some of the things that happened to me while you were gone. First, Gertrude Jenkins showed up."

"Yes, I remember passing her on the way down the drive."

"Well, she came and we were introduced, and your name came up." She paused and looked away. Why couldn't this just be simple? *Because you're making it harder than it has to be,* Jessica's heart told her.

She held up her hand. "None of that is important. The truth is, I love you." She turned to see what his reaction might be. "It terrifies me in a way I can't even begin to explain, but that's the truth, and I thought from something Kate had told me that you might be given to feeling the same way. Then when I saw you coming home, I just forgot myself and let my heart take over. I'm sorry."

"Truly?"

She shook her head in confusion. "Truly what?"

"You're truly sorry? Sorry you let your heart guide you? Sorry you threw yourself into my arms and kissed me?" He stepped

253

closer and reached his hand up to touch her cheek.

Jessica felt her breath quicken. "No."

"No?" he questioned, the tiniest grin causing his mustache to rise.

Jessica lifted her chin ever so slightly. "No, I'm not sorry. I'm powerfully embarrassed, but I'm not sorry."

"Why are you embarrassed?"

"Because I made a fool of myself," Jessica replied. "Something I seem to do quite a bit when you're around."

This made Devon laugh. "If this is you being a fool, then I like it, and I wouldn't have you change a single thing. But I don't think this is foolish."

"No?" It was Jessica's turn to question.

He moved his face closer to hers, and she knew without a doubt he would kiss her. Could it be, her mind reeled, that he did return her feelings? Was it possible he loved her?

"You never gave me much of a chance to speak to you on the matter," he whispered, his breath warm on her face. "I don't think being in love is foolish. Especially when both people feel the same way."

She felt her eyes grow wide. "Truly?" She found herself repeating the very word he'd used earlier. "You love me?"

"I do," he murmured. "And I'd like to respond to your earlier greeting."

His lips closed upon hers, and his arms pulled her tightly into his embrace. Jessica's knees grew weak. She embraced the overwhelming joy that flooded her heart and soul. It seemed impossible that Devon was standing there, saying the things he was saying, kissing her as he was kissing her, but it also seemed so right. Jessica thought it felt perfect, as if they were meant for each other.

Devon kissed her lips, then let his kisses trail up her cheek to her eyebrow and then to her forehead. Jessica sighed and put her head against his shoulder.

"You know, you seem to make a habit of kissing men you aren't engaged to," he whispered.

Jessica laughed and pulled away. "Then maybe you'd better rectify the situation."

He smiled. "I'd be happy to." He pulled out a ring from his pocket. "This belonged to my grandmother. It's the same one I gave to Jane and the same one she brought back to me. But it's special to me, and I hope you'll overlook her involvement with it. This ring was worn by my grandmother for some fifty-seven years of marriage. She adored my grandfather, and he adored her. I want that kind of marriage, Jess. I want that for us. Will you accept this ring and my proposal of marriage?"

Tears coursed down Jessica's face. She took the ring and slipped it on her finger. It fit perfectly, the little carved gold band glittering in the moonlight. "The past is gone, but this ring will be a reminder to us both of what true love can endure and accomplish. I've prayed for this, asked God to send me the kind of man who could be a father to my son, as well as a husband to me." She looked up from the ring to meet Devon's passionate gaze. "Yes, I'll marry you."

EPILOGUE

June 1892

Ryan danced circles around his parents. Devon and Jessica Carter laughed to see the spectacle the small boy was creating.

"People comin' to see me," he said happily. "Dey comin' now."

"Yes, son," Devon said, scooping the boy up into his arms. "Buck is bringing us a whole bunch of people." He rubbed the thick dark curls that covered Ryan's head.

"I hope we aren't making a mistake," Jessica said, nervously twisting her hands. She'd been married less than two months to Devon, and now they were opening Windridge as a resort ranch. "I mean, maybe you were right. Maybe we should never have let this thing get this far."

Devon eyed her with a raised brow and laughed. "Now you're willing to listen to me?"

Jessica shook her head. "Oh Devon, did

we make the wrong decision?" She could see the stage approaching and knew that within a few minutes, total strangers would descend on their steps.

"Remember why you thought to do this in the first place?"

Jessica nodded. "I thought it would make a quiet respite."

"Not only that, but you saw it as the perfect opportunity to share God with other folks."

"But what if they don't like it here?"

Devon shrugged. "What if they don't? We have the partnership intact with the Rocking W, and it'll only be another year or so before we're completely solvent."

"Maybe we shouldn't have taken on all those cattle," Jessica said. "I mean you had to hire all those hands, and now we've got these people coming and —"

Devon put his finger to her lips, and Ryan leaned over to follow suit by placing his pudgy hand against her mouth. "Mama, peoples comin' to see me."

Jessica pulled back and smiled. "All right. I get your point. We can't do anything about it now. The guests are already here."

"Exactly. Let's give it a try. We've got a full summer ahead of us with plenty of folks who want to see what a dude ranch is all about. Let's just wait and see what happens. We might both be so happy to be done with it by the end of summer that we'll never even want to consider doing this another year."

"I suppose you're right," Jessica replied.

"I've no doubt people will find this place a blessing," Devon said. "I know I have."

Jessica sighed. "So have I."

Buck approached with the stage-styled carriage and brought the horses to a stop not ten feet from the front walk.

"Well, they're here," Devon said, shifting Ryan in his arms.

"Peoples here, Mama!" Ryan called and clapped his hands.

Jessica laughed at his enthusiasm. Through the open windows of the carriage, Jessica could hear animated conversation between the passengers. She couldn't make out the words, but knew that soon enough she'd probably hear plenty from her guests. Just then, Buck scrambled down from the driver's seat and positioned the stepping platform for the passengers. The door opened, and to Jessica's surprise the passengers poured out arguing — bickering over something that Jessica couldn't quite make out.

"Well, here are your people," Devon said, leaning close to whisper. "Looks like they could use a good dose of peace and quiet."

She nodded. "I suppose we'd better welcome them before they kill each other."

She stepped forward and rang a triangular bell that hung at the edge of the porch. The metallic ring caused everyone to fall into silence and give her their full attention.

Jessica gave them what she hoped was her friendliest smile. "Good afternoon. I'm Jessica Carter, and this is my husband, Devon, and son, Ryan. We'd like to welcome you to the house on Windridge."

ABOUT THE AUTHOR

Tracie Peterson, bestselling, award-winning author of over ninety fiction titles and three non-fiction books, lives and writes in Belgrade, Montana. As a Christian, wife, mother, writer, editor, and speaker (in that order), Tracie finds her slate quite full.

Published in magazines and Sunday school take home papers, as well as a columnist for a Christian newspaper, Tracie now focuses her attention on novels. After signing her first contract with Barbour Publishing in 1992, her novel, *A Place To Belong,* appeared in 1993 and the rest is history. She has over twenty-six titles with Heartsong Presents' book club (many of which have been repackaged) and stories in six separate anthologies from Barbour. From Bethany House Publishing, Tracie has multiple historical three-book series as well as many stand-alone contemporary women's fiction stories and two non-fiction titles.

Other titles include two historical series co-written with Judith Pella, one historical series co-written with James Scott Bell, and multiple historical series co-written with Judith Miller.

The employees of Thorndike Press hope you have enjoyed this Large Print book. All our Thorndike, Wheeler, and Kennebec Large Print titles are designed for easy reading, and all our books are made to last. Other Thorndike Press Large Print books are available at your library, through selected bookstores, or directly from us.

For information about titles, please call:
   (800) 223-1244

or visit our Web site at:
   http://gale.cengage.com/thorndike

To share your comments, please write:
   Publisher
   Thorndike Press
   10 Water St., Suite 310
   Waterville, ME 04901